HOPE
DOESN'T DISAPPOINT

HOPE
DOESN'T DISAPPOINT

DORALYN MOORE

COPYRIGHT NOTICE

Hope Doesn't Disappoint

First edition. Copyright © 2022 by Doralyn Moore. The information contained in this book is the intellectual property of Doralyn Moore and is governed by United States and International copyright laws. All rights reserved. No part of this publication, either text or image, may be used for any purpose other than personal use. Therefore, reproduction, modification, storage in a retrieval system, or retransmission, in any form or by any means, electronic, mechanical, or otherwise, for reasons other than personal use, except for brief quotations for reviews or articles and promotions, is strictly prohibited without prior written permission by the publisher.

This is a work of fiction. Names, characters, businesses, places, events, locales, and incidents are either the products of the author's imagination or used in a fictitious manner. Any resemblance to actual persons, living or dead, or actual events is purely coincidental.

Scripture taken from the THE HOLY BIBLE, ENGLISH STANDARD VERSION (ESV): Scriptures taken from THE HOLY BIBLE, ENGLISH STANDARD VERSION ® Copyright© 2001 by Crossway, a publishing ministry of Good News Publishers. Used by permission.

Scripture taken from THE LIVING BIBLE copyright© 1971. Used by permission of Tyndale House Publishers, Inc., Carol Stream, Illinois 60188. All rights reserved.

Scripture taken from the THE MESSAGE: THE BIBLE IN CONTEMPORARY ENGLISH (TM): Scripture taken from THE MESSAGE: THE BIBLE IN CONTEMPORARY ENGLISH, copyright©1993, 1994, 1995, 1996, 2000, 2001, 2002. Used by permission of NavPress Publishing Group

Scripture quotations marked TPT are from The Passion Translation®. Copyright © 2017, 2018, 2020 by Passion & Fire Ministries, Inc. Used by permission. All rights reserved. ThePassionTranslation.com.

Cover and Interior Design: Jeff Gifford (Gradient), Derinda Babcock, Deb Haggerty

Editor(s): Mary W. Johnson, Cristel Phelps, Deb Haggerty

PUBLISHED BY: Elk Lake Publishing, Inc., 35 Dogwood Drive, Plymouth, MA 02360, 2022

Library Cataloging Data

Names: Moore, Doralyn (Doralyn Moore)

Hope Doesn't Disappoint / Doralyn Moore

238 p. 23cm × 15cm (9in × 6 in.)

ISBN-13: 978-1-64949-572-3 (paperback) | 978-1-64949-573-0 (trade paperback) | 978-1-64949-574-7 (e-book)

Key Words: Gambling; Addiction; Support Groups; Marriage; Second Chances; Redemption; Family

Library of Congress Control Number: 2022937812 Fiction

DEDICATION

This book is dedicated to my husband, Carey. Your love and encouragement mean everything to me. Thank you, sweetheart.

ACKNOWLEDGMENTS

Thank you to Deb Haggerty, Cristel Phelps, and Mary Johnson. Your many skills and willingness to help are deeply appreciated.

I would also like to acknowledge my mother, Dorothy Lillian Nesbitt, who is now in Heaven with Jesus. She helped me with the research for the book.

CHAPTER ONE

We may toss the coin and roll the dice, but God's will is greater than luck. Proverbs 16:33 (TPT)

Cassie scanned the evidence of how the conditions of her life had deteriorated as the weather had changed from a high wind advisory to a Category 3 hurricane. Papers, dirty clothes, green garbage bags full of odds and ends, Styrofoam coffee cups, and chocolate bar wrappers littered the back seat of her Honda Accord, spreading a thin layer of grime over her once pristine leather seats. A bashed-in tissue box lay on the passenger side, half-hidden under her purse and a cheap paperback novel. The car reeked of stale onions and coagulated grease. She was homeless and almost penniless. There wasn't much more that could be blown away. Resting her head on the steering wheel, she closed her eyes, blocking out her chaotic life.

Several minutes passed before she raised her head and stared at the house across the street. Bed sheets covered the two front windows. A shiny new lock had been installed on the front door. A rusty dumpster hulked in the driveway, with wood, bricks, metal pipes, and other debris visible over the top.

The sheriff's notice was still in the front window. Torn, faded, blowing in the wind, it announced to the world the bank's foreclosure on the previous owners.

Studying her former home—perhaps soon to be renovated and sold to strangers—deepened Cassie's despair. All she had now were the memories of the years she and her family had lived there. At least no one could take those.

Nothing else in the neighborhood had changed. The grounds of the Taylor house next door were still beautifully manicured, and as usual, elderly Mrs. Hutchinson sat in her rocking chair on her front porch, her dog curled at her feet.

Rolling down the window, Cassie breathed in the fragrance of the warm spring day. The cherry tree in their old front lawn had blossomed, scattering a blanket of snowy white petals on the grass beneath it. Overgrown grass and weeds concealed the front walk, but bits and pieces of the interlocking pathway poked through.

A picture of her daughters—eight-year-old Anne-Marie and five-year-old Jesse—selling lemonade at the end of the walkway flooded Cassie's mind, making her laugh and cry at the same time. Anne-Marie had sat soberly behind the table, counting their change, and making sure they were well stocked with cups and napkins. Jesse, never able to sit still, had run up and down the street searching for customers, her braids bobbing in the breeze. Passing neighbors had been generous in their purchases. When the girls counted their money at day's end, they had earned a total of eight dollars and forty cents. As soon as Cassie gave them permission, they raced off to the neighborhood convenience store to purchase ice cream cones.

Cassie closed her eyes and rubbed her throbbing temples. The pain of missing her daughters was agony, both mental and physical.

The clattering roar of an engine in urgent need of a new muffler attracted Cassie's attention. A red pick-up truck stopped briefly in front of the house, then turned into the driveway. A tall, thin man got out of the truck and walked to the front door. Removing a key from his pocket, he unlocked the door and slipped inside.

Taking a deep breath, Cassie slid lower in her seat. Half an hour passed before the man banged the front door open and descended the front steps to his truck. He fished around in the back and finally pulled out a power sander. Refinishing the hardwood floors would probably be a wise decision if he wanted to sell the house quickly. The floors had certainly seen their share of wear.

The morning breeze carried the fragrance of freshly mowed grass. The scent soothed Cassie, and she closed her eyes and drifted back into memories.

A knuckle-knock on the driver's side door startled her awake, and she glanced at her watch. She'd been asleep a good forty-five minutes. Groggy and disoriented, she looked up into the face of a police officer.

She did a quick face check in the side view mirror. The hours she had spent sitting on park benches in the sunshine had added tinges of blonde to her light brown hair. The shape of her ear-length cut had long since disappeared and become ragged. She definitely did not look her best. Then she examined the officer standing next to her.

She judged him to be about five feet, five inches tall, the same as her own height. His small, piercing brown eyes, straight black hair, and slightly crooked narrow nose reminded her of an eagle ready to swoop down on its prey.

"What is it, Officer?" Cassie felt sweat on her face. His name tag said Officer G. Brownlow.

"Somebody reported a suspicious car in the neighborhood, and I came to check it out. What are you doing here?"

"I guess you could say I'm cruising down memory lane. I used to live in this area."

"Well, it's time to move on. Neighbors don't like it when someone sits in their car for no apparent reason." The policeman's eyes narrowed. "I need to see your driver's license, registration, and proof of insurance, ma'am."

Cassie's fingers shook as she picked up her purse and rifled through it, looking for her wallet. Finally locating it, she dug out her license, registration, and insurance and handed them to the officer. Without a word, he took her documents and walked back to his cruiser.

Massaging her temples, Cassie breathed a sigh of relief she had made her monthly car insurance payment with her father's money.

The officer spent an inordinate amount of time going over her information. When he finally returned, his expression appeared set in granite. "You have a bench warrant for outstanding fines. I'll have to take you in."

"A what?"

"A bench warrant. Nine hundred and fifty dollars in unpaid parking tickets."

All the air blew out of Cassie in a rush. She had hoped the unpaid parking tickets, low on her priority list of bills to pay, would catch up with her later rather than sooner.

"You have to take me in for unpaid parking tickets?" Her tone reverberated at an octave higher than normal.

Brownlow nodded and motioned for Cassie to get out of the car. She opened the door and stood up slowly. After frisking her, he took her by the elbow and propelled her toward the cruiser.

"I'll pay those tickets as soon as I can, Officer. You don't have to take me to the station." Cassie dragged her feet, making it difficult for Brownlow to move her along.

Brownlow unfastened a clip on his belt and dangled a pair of handcuffs in Cassie's face. "Do I have to use these?"

A tear rolled down Cassie's cheek and splattered onto her stained sweatshirt.

"No," she whispered. "Please don't use those." She watched in relief as Brownlow returned the cuffs to his belt.

At the cruiser, Brownlow opened the back door and pushed Cassie onto the back seat, stained with sweat and who knew what else. The lock clicked. She was trapped. A cage separated her from Brownlow. Beads of perspiration dotted her forehead, and her pounding heart hammered in her ears.

He signed onto his radio. "I'm transporting a female to the station. My starting mileage is ..."

As they pulled away, Cassie saw Nancy Hesser, the neighbor three doors down, watching from her front porch. They had been best friends until Cassie started borrowing money she couldn't repay. Cassie's cheeks burned, and her eyes filled with fresh tears. Nancy had seen Officer Brownlow shove her inside the cruiser like a common criminal.

Voices crackled over the police radio, grating on Cassie's taut nerves as they drove from her previous little corner of Kettering to a part of town she wasn't well acquainted with.

Cassie sat up straighter when Brownlow pulled up to a yellow brick building with a triangular, glassed-in area on the roof, and numerous antennae on its top. Brownlow maneuvered down the narrow driveway at the back of the building and stopped in front of a closed garage door. Several seconds passed before the door opened automatically. They drove inside, and the metal barrier shut with a thud behind them.

Brownlow brought the car to a stop, hopped out, and opened the rear door.

"Out." Cassie's legs trembled as her feet touched the ground.

She followed Brownlow through a heavy steel door into an L-shaped room with a partitioned area on one side. A bench ran the length of one wall. Motioning for Cassie to sit on the bench, Brownlow entered the partitioned area to talk to another officer, who listened and then nodded.

"I've got it from here." The other officer waved Brownlow out, and he strode from the room, giving Cassie a curt nod.

"I'm Officer Gord Whelan."

Cassie jumped. Distracted, she'd not heard him approach. Now he stared down at her. "I need to verify your information before assigning you to a cell."

Cassie shook her head, her eyes wide in disbelief. Blood rushed in her ears.

Whelan stated Cassie's full name and date of birth, and she nodded. Then he read out her previous address.

"I don't live there anymore." She spoke so softly Whelan leaned closer. "I, uh—" She stopped and stared at Whelan.

He waited.

"I don't …" Tears welled in Cassie's eyes, and her voice cracked. "I don't have an address."

"Okay." Whelan picked up a telephone receiver and punched a number. "Can you send a female officer to the holding area, please? Thanks."

A tear fell from Cassie's eye, and she searched in her purse for a tissue but couldn't find one. Wiping her nose with the sleeve of her sweatshirt, she sat back and tried to think who she could call to help her. Nausea rose from the pit of her stomach.

A tall female officer with clear blue eyes, a freckled nose, and blonde hair tied back in a ponytail entered the room.

"She hasn't been searched yet," Whelan said.

The female officer took Cassie to a private enclosure. She did a thorough job of searching Cassie from her hair downward, and Cassie's face grew hot with embarrassment. Afterward, she told Cassie to remove her belt and shoelaces. The trembling in her hands made it difficult for her to work her shoelaces out of her shoes. When she finally managed it, the officer reached out, took the items, placed them in a bag, and labeled it before depositing the bag inside one of the lockers hanging on the wall. She led Cassie back out to where Officer Whelan waited.

"I'm done," the female officer said, and left the room.

As soon as the woman left, Whelan asked Cassie to show him her purse. Handing him her frayed, torn bag, she watched as he turned it upside down onto the counter, allowing stray pieces of paper, a bankbook, a lipstick tube, a ballpoint pen, a worn out toothbrush, a half-empty toothpaste container, a comb, and four quarters to tumble out.

He picked up the quarters and held them in his hand. "Is this all the money you have?"

"There's a five-dollar bill in the zippered pocket at the back."

After checking the back of Cassie's purse, Whelan entered the information into his computer, printed out a form, and pushed it in Cassie's direction.

"Sign here that you brought six dollars with you," he said, writing a big X at the bottom of the page and thumping his index finger on the line.

Cassie's fingers shook so badly she could barely write her name. Whelan then entered her property into the computer and printed out another form, which he shoved in front of Cassie for her signature. Next, he placed her purse and its contents into the bag inside the locker.

Pointing to a laminated sign on the wall, Whelan asked Cassie to read it aloud.

"You have the right to retain and instruct counsel without delay," she read slowly, doing her best to concentrate. "You have the right to telephone any lawyer you wish. You also have the right to free advice from a legal aid lawyer. If you are charged with an offense, you may apply to the Legal Aid Plan for assistance. The toll-free numbers listed below will put you into contact with a Legal Aid Duty Counsel Lawyer for free legal advice right now."

"Do you understand what you just read?" Whelan scrutinized Cassie closely.

Cassie nodded.

"Do you want to call a lawyer now?"

Cassie nodded again.

"You can use that phone." He pointed to one sitting on a nearby desk.

Cassie called the first number listed. As she punched it out, humiliation swept over her at the thought of telling a stranger how she ended up in a police station with a warrant issued against her for unpaid parking tickets.

After five rings, a clipped voice answered. "Suzanne Graziano. How can I help you?"

Cassie sobbed as if a dam had burst inside her. Neither woman spoke while Cassie tried desperately to regain her composure. Finally she blurted out, "I'm being held at the police station because I can't pay my parking tickets."

"How much do you owe?"

"Nine hundred and fifty dollars."

Suzanne whistled through her teeth. "My goodness, that's an awful lot of parking tickets. How did you rack up that many?"

Cassie took a deep breath before answering. "It's a long story."

"Can you pay them, or do you know someone who could pay it for you?"

"Maybe someone who could. No one who would."

"Family, friends, neighbors, business associates, even acquaintances?" Ms. Graziano stopped. "Anyone?"

"No." The word came out as a wail.

"There must be someone who can help you."

Cassie didn't answer.

"What station are you booked into?"

HOPE DOESN'T DISAPPOINT

"Number Five, I think. The one on Larkin Avenue."

"You're right. The one on Larkin is Station Five." The noise of rustling papers came through the phone. "Look, I'm not far from there. I'm in the middle of something, but I'll do my best to come over in an hour or so."

"Thank you," Cassie whispered. She hung up the phone and rubbed her temples, the pain worse than ever.

Whelan was waiting. "I'll assign you to a cell." After banging a few keys on the computer, he motioned toward the far end of the room. "Cell Four. Down that way."

Hesitantly, Cassie walked toward the steel door with a black 4 painted on it, with Whelan behind her. He opened the cell door, and Cassie stepped inside.

The room looked to be approximately eight feet by five feet. A stainless-steel sink and toilet stood at one end. A fiberglass bench which served as a bed protruded from the wall. The only window was the sliding one in the door. The place reeked of sweat and vomit. She walked to the bench and sat down.

Seconds later, the lock clicked home, and Whelan's footsteps thumped on the terrazzo tile as he walked away. Cold and sore from the hard seat, Cassie fought to breathe as her chest tightened. Whelan had mercifully left the window open, and Cassie stood and peeked through it, seeing only a grim landscape of concrete and metal. No sound echoed in the cell area except the occasional disembodied voice of the public address system. Could she be the only one in lock-up? The thought sent a sharp chill down her spine.

Cassie looked around the room for something to help occupy her time, but there was nothing. Unsure what to do next, she removed her shoes and lay down with her back on the bed. The hard surface pressed against her shoulder blades, and her head fell too far back, hurting her neck. Feeling totally drained, she closed her eyes.

"There's someone here to see you."

Cassie jerked and looked up, saw Officer Whelan, and realized she'd fallen asleep. Fear hit her like a tidal wave, threatening to drown her. Sitting up slowly, she rubbed her shoulders and neck and swung her feet over the side of the bench.

"You can talk in the interview room."

Cassie took a deep breath to calm herself, stood, slipped on her shoes, and waited by the door for Whelan to unlock it. When the lock clicked, she stepped out into the hallway. The bright lights stunned her. Through the glare, she saw a tall, thin, middle-aged woman with large brown eyes staring at her.

The woman's hair was ear-length and fashionably cut, framing an oval face. She wore black pants with a matching jacket over a black and white print silk blouse. The ankle boots she sported were probably Jimmy Choos.

Whelan quickly made the introductions. "This is Suzanne Graziano." He glanced back at Cassie. "I believe you've asked her to be your counsel." Nodding at Cassie, he said to the lawyer, "This is Cassandra Bailey."

"You can call me Cassie."

Ms. Graziano nodded and motioned for Cassie to follow her into a room with two chairs placed at a circular table. Cassie's nostrils twitched. The room smelled musty and stale. The gray walls and carpet did nothing to lift her spirits. After the women took seats, the lawyer squinted at the legal pad she had removed from her briefcase and placed it on the table next to her cell phone. "The information I have says you don't live at the address on file for you. She glanced over at Cassie.

HOPE DOESN'T DISAPPOINT

"Um ..." Cassie hesitated and looked down at her hands. "I ... uh ... don't have an address."

"So you're homeless."

"Well, not exactly. I'm ... living ... out ..." Cassie took a deep breath. "... of my car for now." She mumbled the last words, hoping the lawyer wouldn't hear them.

Ms. Graziano leaned forward and placed her hands on the table. Cassie couldn't help noticing her manicured fingernails. She glanced at her own nails, chewed to the quick, and curled her fingers under as the lawyer spoke.

"Do you have a history of mental health issues or substance abuse concerns?"

Cassie shook her head.

"Why don't you have a fixed address?" Her eyes searched Cassie's face.

Cassie repositioned herself on the chair. "I told you before. It's a long story." She kept her eyes focused on the table.

"I finished what I needed to get done before I arrived here, so I've got time." Ms. Graziano glanced at her phone and leaned back in her chair.

Seconds passed before Cassie spoke. Her eyes brimmed with tears that tracked down her cheeks no matter how she tried to stop them.

"You have to understand my life was pretty normal before all the mayhem began." Cassie stopped and inhaled. "It all began a year ago this spring. I guess my story begins then." She looked down at her hands.

"It took a while for me to end up homeless."

CHAPTER TWO

"I have to go out of town for two days," Cassie announced. She stood in the family room and watched her husband, Jon, flip between television channels. Stray books and magazines lay scattered on the floor, and she bent to pick them up. Outside the window, the sky had darkened, and a hard wind rattled the panes. It looked like they might be in for a storm later in the evening. The weather had been dry lately. Rain would be good for the farmers' crops.

It took a moment for Jon to respond as he switched to yet another network.

"Okay. Is Aunt Nellie available for the girls?" Although not related by blood, Aunt Nellie was a long-time friend who seemed like family. She had looked after Anne-Marie and Jesse when the girls were small, so Cassie could return to work.

"She's available." Cassie frowned as she sat down beside him. "You know, I love being a buyer for Bigelows, but I hate the travel part because I have to be away from you and the kids."

"It's only two days." Jon patted Cassie's knee. "Just as long as Nellie's available, we'll be fine." After watching TV for a few seconds, he sniffed the air. "Hmm, something smells good. What's for dinner tonight?"

"Roasted chicken, potatoes, peas, and a salad."

"Sounds good. What about dessert?"

Cassie punched him playfully in the arm. "Not asking for much, are you?"

"My wife always delivers." He pecked her on the cheek.

"To answer your last question, we're having apple crisp." She stood and entered the kitchen. An aroma of perfectly roasted chicken wafted in the air as she removed the roasting pan and set it on the counter. At the door, she called the girls to come in for dinner.

"Just one more game of hopscotch." Jesse picked up her marker and threw it on the first square.

"No more games," Cassie said sternly. "Inside. Now."

Jesse took two hops before she looked up. "All right, we're coming," she said reluctantly. Anne-Marie had already picked up her marker and was heading for the house.

By the time the girls washed their hands, Cassie had set out the meal.

"Dinner's on the table."

The handwash splashing from the main floor bathroom let her know Jon had heard her.

Knives and forks scraped against porcelain as the family dived into their meal. Halfway through, Jon set his fork down and looked around the table.

"How are the three prettiest girls in the world? Did you all have a good day?"

"Mom's not a girl." Anne-Marie and Jesse giggled when they both spoke in unison.

Jon flashed a big smile. "She's my girl."

Jesse's smile faded, and she looked down. "My day wasn't so good."

"Why not?"

"I got ten out of twenty on my arithmetic."

Cassie grimaced. "Uh-oh, looks like someone is going to be spending more time on their homework in the evenings and less time watching television."

HOPE DOESN'T DISAPPOINT

"I knew you'd say that." Jesse scowled at her mother.

"How about you, Anne-Marie? How was your day?"

Anne-Marie finished chewing before answering. "I was asked to play one of my pieces on the piano for the school talent night," she said shyly.

"That's wonderful!" Cassie exclaimed. Jon reached over and gave Anne-Marie's shoulder a congratulatory pat.

"Well, I had a good day, too," he said. "Naturally, sales managers get incentives for the dealership to sell more cars. My group sold the most cars for the month. That means I get an extra bonus." Jon stood up and danced a little jig, pumping his arms in the air.

The children cheered, and Cassie got up from her seat to plant a juicy kiss on her husband's cheek. "My hero."

"That just leaves you, Mom. How was your day?"

"My day was good." Cassie smiled, but then her smile turned into a frown. "The only bad thing is I have to travel for two days next week."

The girls groaned. "Is Aunt Nellie coming?"

"She is." Cassie gave the girls a pointed stare. "And I want a good report from her about you two when I get home."

Her severity was an act, and they knew it. The girls were rarely in trouble, and her husband was the best. If only she didn't have to travel so often.

The day Cassie had to leave for her business trip to Ottawa arrived sooner than she would have liked. She arrived at the hotel, tired from the drive, and found she'd been booked into what looked like a new Hudson Suites hotel constructed totally of steel and glass, rising high enough to need blinking red lights on the roof to warn off aircraft. Check-in was effortless, and when Cassie arrived in her room, everything smelled new. The room's tasteful design in neutral grays and pops of blue reminded her of home.

She sat on the edge of the bed and turned on the television. After scanning all the channels and finding nothing which captured her attention, she decided to go for a walk. Perhaps it would renew her energy.

When Cassie reached the hotel's ground floor, a flock of people were headed in the same direction down one of the hotel corridors. She followed them to a large convention-sized room where rows of slot machines occupied half the area. Blackjack and roulette tables filled another section. A sign over a doorway leading to a smaller room announced the game of baccarat.

Interesting. The hotel actually had its own casino.

People of all sorts—young, old, middle-aged, slim, trim, overweight, and everything in between—perched on tall stools, staring at the brightly lit slot machines. The only thing they had in common was their high degree of concentration on the screens in front of them.

An elderly lady near the door had her purse propped on a walker beside her. She repeatedly pressed the button on her console, her eyes unblinking. Without warning, electronic lights flashed, a tinny fanfare blared, and a voice announced, "Congratulations! You've won the jackpot!" The lady flung her flaccid arms into the air and grinned, revealing two missing teeth.

More electronic music blared from the back of the room. Cassie walked over to see the fortunate person who had won. A tall man with dark hair and a pronounced beer belly pushed himself to his feet.

"Congratulations," Cassie said.

"It's been a long time coming." He smiled. "But better late than never."

"For sure."

"You playing?"

"Maybe next time." Cassie waved and headed to the coffee shop for a cup of herbal tea.

She daydreamed as she idly stirred her tea at the coffee shop's tiny table. She couldn't get the excitement of seeing someone win a jackpot out of her mind. Winning a jackpot would be like putting a big maraschino cherry on top of a successful buying trip.

The show's final two days flew by. Bigelows was well known for its high-end furniture, and Cassie always found it challenging to predict future trends and choose items which would be in vogue months down the road. And although she enjoyed the trips, they exhausted her. She drove home with the car window down and the radio blaring to make sure she stayed awake.

When she arrived home in the late afternoon, Aunt Nellie had everything under control. The girls were busy doing their homework, and delicious kitchen aromas floated in the air. Nellie met her at the front door.

"Welcome home. How was your trip?"

"Demanding but rewarding. I think I made some good buys." Cassie set her luggage in the front hall and hung up her coat "Something sure smells good."

"Meat loaf, baked potatoes, and cauliflower with cheese sauce."

"Will you stay for dinner with us, Nellie?"

Nellie shook her head. "My daughter's bringing her two children over after they eat. Her husband's away on a business trip. While the kiddos do their homework, Jodi and I are going to do some macrame. She designs home interiors, and she needs a special statement piece for one wall."

"Well, I wish you success."

"Thanks, we'll need it. Especially if the kids start to get antsy." Nellie slipped on her coat and picked up her overnight bag and purse. "Do you know when your next trip is?"

Cassie shook her head. "No, but as soon as I know, you'll know." She pulled an envelope from her purse. In addition to Nellie's pay, she'd also included a thank-you card decorated with bright flowers.

"Thank you, Cassie." Nellie slipped the envelope into her pocket and departed with a little wave. Cassie waved back and watched Nellie move down the front walkway to her car, then head down the street.

Later that night, Cassie sat in her bedroom on a chair by the window, holding Jesse's report card in her hand. Jon was stretched out on the bed, his back against pillows lined up against the headboard, thumbing through a fitness magazine.

"Beside Jesse's C in French, the teacher wrote, 'Jesse understands sentence structure and is making progress in her vocabulary, but she loses interest easily. More attention to detail is required.' And that's not all. The notation next to her C minus in arithmetic is that Jesse needs to put forth a more serious effort and to complete the assignments on time."

"That sounds normal, especially for Jesse."

"Most of her grades on this report are C's. Last term she got a lot more B's. I'm worried."

Jon stopped turning magazine pages and glanced in Cassie's direction. "I think you're making a big deal about nothing, Cass. All kids go through slumps in their schoolwork. Didn't you?"

"No, I did not."

"Well, I did, and I turned out all right." Jon crossed his eyes and laughed. Cassie ignored him.

"I think we should take her out of the public system and put her into a private school."

"It's not necessary, Cass."

"I'm going to start looking into private schools tomorrow. One of the women at work sends her kids to a private school. I'll ask her which one."

"We're not sending Jesse to a private school. For one thing, she doesn't need it. And secondly, we can't afford it."

Rather than start an argument, Cassie headed to the bathroom, took a hot shower, and prepared for bed. When she returned to the bedroom thirty minutes later, Jon was on his side, snoring loudly, the magazine on the floor where he'd tossed it. Cassie slipped into the bed beside him. Even with her frustration about his opinion on Jesse's schooling, she knew at his core he always wanted what was best for his family.

Cassie regarded him while he slept. She had to admire his drive and determination, traits which probably made him such a good sales manager. She couldn't help smiling at the memory of the summer he hired her for a job painting houses. She'd seen his determination then. He told her he worked his team hard so they could win best painting team competitions. He scowled at her outfit and asked her if she'd ever done any painting before. When she said no, he turned and walked away. When she told him she learned fast, he returned but didn't look too happy.

She'd liked his tall, muscular body, the sandy color of his hair, the freckles sprinkled across his cheeks and nose, the cleft in his chin. What she didn't like was his attitude. She'd been surprised when he employed her.

Cassie's eyes grew heavy. Those days were long past. Where had the time gone?

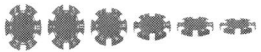

The next week passed uneventfully. After a relaxing weekend, on Monday morning, chaos reigned as usual,. Cassie sighed with relief as she watched the girls climb onto their school bus. Hastily, she picked up miscellaneous items scattered in the hallway. A glance at the clock told her she'd better hurry if she hoped to get to work on time.

Jon entered the kitchen and pecked her on the cheek. He wore a navy suit with a light blue shirt and tie. His hair was still wet from the shower.

"You look nice today," Cassie said.

"You do too."

Cassie laughed, looking down at her faded bathrobe, nondescript nightgown, and ragged slippers.

Jon filled a thermos with coffee from the coffeemaker. "I don't have time for breakfast this morning." He grabbed two cookies from the cookie jar before heading out.

"Wait a minute," Cassie called. "Just to give you a heads up. I'm going out of town for a couple of days next week, to the same place I went on my last trip. A new shipment has come in. Aunt Nellie's all …"

Cassie could hear Jon snap his fingers as he returned to the doorway. "Sorry. I forgot to tell you. Melanie from your work called and told me about the trip. Said she's booked you into the same hotel as before. I hope that's okay."

Cassie nodded.

"Gotta run." Jon blew a kiss and slammed the front door behind him as he left.

Cassie hurried up the stairs to get ready for work. The idea of being at the hotel with the casino stuck pleasantly in her head. At work, the memory of the sights and sounds of the gaming room periodically flashed through her mind, distracting her.

A whirlwind of work, keeping the children on track for school, preparing meals, and trying to get her family to clean up after themselves made the remainder of the week slip by quickly. Before she knew it, she had to set out again on her business trip.

The hotel was as pristine as ever. She was given a different room from the previous time, a larger one with green draperies and bed coverings rather than neutral-colored. She liked the green better. As soon as she was settled, she picked up her cell phone and punched in her home number. The phone rang and rang before a childish voice finally came over the wire.

"Hello?"

"Jesse, it's Mom. How are you?"

"Good."

"How was school today? I missed you."

"I missed you too, Mom." Jesse didn't say anything, and Cassie wondered if she was all right. Several seconds passed before she spoke again. "I had a good day today. Elizabeth invited me to her birthday party on Saturday. Can I go?"

When Cassie didn't answer right away, Jesse begged, "Please, please?"

"I think so, but I'm not making any promises. Is Daddy home from work yet?"

"Nope, but Aunt Nellie made his favorite for supper—pot pie. She said he can heat it up in the microwave when he gets home."

"Sounds good. Can I speak to Aunt Nellie, Jess?"

Jesse yelled Aunt Nellie's name. Cassie cringed at the volume coming through the phone.

"Hello."

Cassie smiled when she heard the older woman's voice. "I just called to say good night to the girls. How are you, and how are they?"

"We're just fine, Cassie. Don't you worry yourself about us."

"It took a long time for someone to answer the phone. Were you and the girls busy?"

Nellie laughed. "We were making a batch of chocolate chip cookies before the girls' bedtime. The oven timer and the telephone rang at the same time, so we got a bit confused. Sorry about that."

Cassie chuckled. "Is Anne-Marie handy?"

"She's right here. I'll say goodbye for now so you can talk to her."

Seconds passed before Cassie heard Anne-Marie's voice.

"Hi, Mom. We made chocolate chip cookies, and the whole kitchen smells really good."

"How do they taste?" In her mind's eye, Cassie saw bits of cookie crumbs covering her daughters' faces.

"Yummy. Jesse and I had three each."

"Oh, no. You two will be swinging from the rafters."

"Aunt Nellie said we could."

"She spoils you." Cassie looked at her watch. "It's past your bedtime. Let me say good night to Jesse before I hang up. Good night to you, Anne-Marie. I love you. Sweet dreams."

"Sleep tight, Mom." Cassie heard Anne-Marie set down the receiver.

Several seconds passed before Jesse spoke into the telephone. "Night, Mom."

"Jesse, you sound as if your mouth is full." She could hear Jesse trying to swallow. "I think you took one more cookie than Aunt Nellie said you could, right?"

"I won't have any more, Mom. Promise."

"Okay, as long as you promise. Love you."

"Love you too."

Jesse hung up the telephone with a bang. Cassie stared at her phone, longing to hug and kiss her girls. Lonely and unsettled after her phone call, she decided to get out of the confines of the room.

HOPE DOESN'T DISAPPOINT

Taking the elevator to the glitzy lobby, she decided to visit the casino. Once inside, she walked around and examined the different slot machines. She could bet anything from one cent to three dollars. A few machines down from where she stood, an elderly gentleman hunched over his console, repeatedly pressing the button with a gnarled index finger. She moved to the empty machine beside him.

"Gonna play?" the older man asked.

Cassie thought a minute. "Sure, why not?"

Loading some money into the machine, she pressed the button several times. When electronic sounds unexpectedly reverberated in her ears, announcing she had won ten free spins, her heart rate kicked up a notch. Maybe she was close to winning a jackpot. When no jackpot appeared, she swore softly.

"Sometimes it takes a while. Keep at it." The man turned his head slightly as he continued to press the button on his machine.

Minutes later, the money she'd loaded was gone and she hadn't won anything. Disappointed, she rose to leave, but stopped when the gentleman spoke again.

"Don't give up yet."

Cassie decided to put in five more dollars and call it quits. The five bucks disappeared quickly, but instead of stopping, she kept loading in more money. When she finally pulled her phone out of her purse and glanced at the display, her eyes widened in shock. "What time is it?"

The aging man glanced at his wrist. "Twelve forty-five."

"Oh, my goodness!" Cassie exclaimed. "I've got to get to bed so I can get up for work tomorrow morning. As soon as this money is gone, I'm outta here."

At one a.m., Cassie hit the jackpot. She found the music, flashing lights, and electronic voice announcing her win intoxicating.

"Congratulations!" her neighbor called, continuing to press his button as he spoke.

Thrilled with her good fortune, Cassie continued to play. At two thirty in the morning, she stopped, reprimanding herself for staying up so late. No more jackpots materialized. She shook her head and looked to see how much money she had left. To her surprise, only twelve dollars remained. Feeling angry at herself for not quitting when she was ahead, she headed for the door.

CHAPTER THREE

In the tiny interview room at the precinct jail, Suzanne Graziano straightened in her chair and stared at Cassie. A chill in the room made Cassie shiver.

"So far, what you've told me doesn't sound so bad. Countless businesspeople gamble when they're away, especially when there's a casino in the hotel where they're staying." The lawyer picked up a pen and started drawing circles on the legal pad in front of her. "In fact, I have a number of lawyer friends who indulge when they travel." Shrugging her shoulders, she added, "No big deal."

"It's what happens inside me when I'm pressing that button and thinking about all the money I'm going to win." Cassie fidgeted with the hem of her shirt. "I forget about everything else—my husband, my kids, the pressures at work—everything."

Suzanne looked up from her doodling. "Sounds as if gambling acts as a tranquilizer for you."

"I can't explain it. I always want to keep going, thinking if I do, I'll win more." *Or win back what I've lost.*

"Can't you just set aside a certain amount of money to gamble with, and when it's gone, you quit?"

"I wish I could," Cassie wailed. "But if I could, I wouldn't be where I am now."

"All I know so far is that you've been living out of your car. What's the rest of the story, Cassie?"

"Well, a month or so later I started going to the local casino each Saturday when Jon took the girls for their piano lessons. I ended up getting in trouble with my bank. The manager really gave it to me."

"What happened?"

The details were as clear in her mind as if they had happened yesterday.

The bank manager, Evelyn Doyle, called her at work and asked her to come into the branch for a "chat." She sat in front of the manager's huge desk like a misbehaving student in the principal's office.

Ms. Doyle looked to be in her late fifties and wore her salt and pepper hair styled in a bob around her longish face. She had piercing gray eyes, with reading glasses propped on top of her head. She reminded Cassie of her fifth-grade teacher, Mrs. Van Zube. That woman had had eyes in the back of her head.

Ms. Doyle pulled her glasses down and readjusted her computer screen.

"Recently your bank account has been constantly overdrawn, and you've gone over your credit protection limit several times. This has never happened before. Do you have an explanation for it?"

"Don't worry, Ms. Doyle. I'll get this straightened out. I've just had a lot of expenses all at one time," Cassie lied.

"Well, for your own good, I think it's a sound idea for us to cut your overdraft limit in half—from one thousand dollars to five hundred."

Bile formed in the pit of Cassie's stomach. "Please don't change it, Ms. Doyle. That overdraft protection is helpful when I have more expenses than usual in a month."

Penetrating gray eyes peered at Cassie.

"We'll leave it at an overdraft protection amount of five hundred dollars for the next three months." Ms. Doyle's words came out like staccato piano notes. "After three months, if there's no problem, then it can be increased."

Cassie nodded and rose to leave. "There'll be no more problems." Her words were hollow even in her own ears.

"Good." Ms. Doyle rose and walked her to the door.

When Cassie returned to work, she had difficulty concentrating. Every time she started a new task, she imagined Ms. Doyle staring at her reprovingly, just like her father did when she didn't measure up to his expectations. Cassie vowed she'd show the old biddy and not even use her overdraft protection. She typed furiously on her keyboard, thoughts coming at her from all directions.

Lorna Nelson, her boss, stopped by her desk and stared. "You're banging on your computer."

Gritting her teeth in frustration, Cassie shook her head. "I want to get this email written. I'm having problems with the wording."

"Need any help?"

"No. Thanks for offering."

As she walked away, Lorna called over her shoulder, "If you change your mind, you know where I am."

Lorna was one of the hardest workers Cassie knew and an excellent mentor. She'd been a great support for Cassie on her way up through the company's buyer training program.

"What are you working on?"

Startled, Cassie recognized the accent and looked up. "How are you, Wumi?"

Wumi Adeola entered the small workstation and sat down in the extra chair. "You look strung out."

Taking a deep breath, Cassie eyed Wumi. Young and ambitious, the young Nigerian had proved herself as a valuable part of the purchasing team, staying on the road, and ahead of the interior decorating curve.

"Just finishing up an email to one of my vendors." Cassie waved a casual hand toward her computer screen. "What are you up to?"

"I just got a lead on a new vendor south of Halifax. I've made an appointment to visit them next week."

Cassie hadn't developed a new vendor in a long time. "Congratulations."

"Thanks." Wumi rose to leave. "Got to run. Don't work too hard." Waggling her fingers, she hastened toward the exit.

Vaguely unsettled, Cassie returned to her computer. Although they specialized in purchasing for distinct elements of the business, Wumi and the other younger buyers presented a clear threat to her chances for future promotion.

"Stay focused, old girl," she whispered, "although I guess thirty-four isn't really old, even by today's standards."

Work settled into its usual rhythm. Over the weeks, after numerous phone calls, Cassie succeeded in developing new buyer contacts. At home, the girls were occupied with school and lessons. Jon spent long hours at the dealership.

One morning, Cassie stood in the kitchen trying to decide how much mess she could clean up before hightailing upstairs to get ready for work. She'd just picked up a dishrag when Jon yelled from the upstairs landing.

"Cassie! Can you take the girls to their piano lessons this Saturday?"

She eyed the sink full of breakfast remnants and shook her head. Saturday was her time to play the slots.

"Can't, Jon," she shouted back, loading dishes into the dishwasher.

"Aw, come on, Cass." His voice carried his exasperation. "My top salesman asked me to play a pickup game of basketball with him and some other guys from work, and we're leaving for the Y right after the showroom closes. And it's right when I usually take the girls to their lessons." Jon clattered downstairs and entered the kitchen. "It's a great way to bond with my staff outside work." He kissed the back of her neck.

Cassie thought fast.

"Sorry, Jon, but I promised Sally I'd help her sort out her mother's clothes and decide which ones should go to charity. She said her mom's closets are so full, she can hardly get the doors closed." Marveling at her easy lies, Cassie added, "She asked me two weeks ago, and I don't want to cancel on her. Sally helped me out a lot when I redecorated our bedroom."

"Couldn't you postpone it for a day or two?"

"I wouldn't feel right canceling on her."

Jon's disappointment was almost tangible, and she nearly relented. But thoughts of the casino shored up her resolve. She did her best to look crestfallen. "Sorry."

Shrugging his shoulders, Jon headed toward the doorway. "Maybe next time."

"Sure." She gave the counter a vigorous swipe for Jon's benefit as he left.

On Saturday afternoon, half an hour before Jon and the girls were to leave for the lessons, Cassie paced up and down the front hallway, her body tingling in anticipation of hitting the slot machines. One by one, Jon, Anne-Marie, and Jesse appeared in the hallway, the girls carrying their lesson materials.

Cassie gave them both a hug and a kiss. Jon stopped in front of Cassie and pointed at his mouth.

"Don't I get any love around here?"

Laughing, Cassie gave him a juicy kiss on the lips.

"Oh, yuck." Jesse made a face, while Anne-Marie turned her head away.

The three headed out the door. "I shouldn't be home any later than ten o'clock," Cassie called, then waved at the car as it backed out.

Once they were gone, Cassie grabbed her coat and purse from the front closet. In the garage, she smiled as she always did at the sight of her Honda with its spotless obsidian blue pearl exterior. She'd fallen in love with it the moment she first saw it in the showroom.

Little stabs of remorse pinged in her brain as she drove to the casino. She'd been selfish not to let Jon go to his pick-up basketball game.

He really doesn't ask for much.

She turned on the car radio to silence the recriminating voice in her head. The music and mindless chatter forced the reflections from her mind.

The casino parking lot was full as usual. She had to drive around for five minutes before finding an empty space. Pulling in quickly before someone else snatched it, she put the car in park, grabbed her purse, and headed for the entrance.

The casino's familiar sights and sounds calmed Cassie. The smell of fried chicken and French fries floated out to her as she passed one of the many restaurants. Her stomach growled, and she remembered she hadn't eaten anything since breakfast. Fighting the urge to stop, she walked briskly toward the slot machines.

I'll grab something before I leave with my winnings.

Not long ago, she'd graduated to the three-dollar slot machines, reasoning she'd win bigger payouts. This day, her favorite three-dollar machine was gloriously vacant, and Cassie hustled over to it and loaded in her money.

HOPE DOESN'T DISAPPOINT

As soon as she sat down and pressed the button to start the bright flashing images on the screen, everything around her faded into the background. The room became silent, and time stopped. The only thing that mattered was the pursuit—and thrill—of winning.

At eight-thirty, Cassie checked her watch, glad to see she still had an hour or so before she had to leave. Forty-five minutes later, at nine-fifteen, she hit a jackpot. She still had time to play a bit more.

When half her winnings were gone, Cassie checked her watch again.

"Eleven-thirty!"

Jon would be worried sick.

Quickly cashing in the remainder of the jackpot, she headed for the exit. She burned rubber through the streets like a race car driver on a road course, and reached home in twenty minutes.

The house felt eerily quiet. Surmising Jon was already asleep, she tiptoed up the stairs. She'd just gotten into her nightgown when he spoke from the bed.

"Where were you?"

She nearly jumped out of her skin. "Don't do that! You scared me. I thought you were asleep."

"Where were you?" he asked again.

"What do you mean, where was I? I was with Sally at her mom's. There was a lot to do. The time just got away from us, that's all."

"When eleven o'clock came and you weren't home, I found Sally's number in your address book and called her. I woke her up."

Oh, great!

"She had no idea what I was talking about when I mentioned sorting her mom's clothes. I made up some excuse and told her I must have misunderstood you."

"I can explain everything." Cassie tried hard to sound more confident than she felt.

Jon had caught her in a barefaced lie.

CHAPTER FOUR

Three o'clock on Friday afternoon had finally arrived, and Ben Gallagher looked wearily at the debris left behind from his last therapy group of the day, the group for addicted gamblers. The neat circle of chairs he had arranged earlier now looked more like a rectangle. The summer sun shone through the window, warming the room despite the air conditioning and casting shadows across the floor.

When he returned to the therapy room after taking the garbage out, Ben arranged the chairs in a proper circle. He was a stickler about the circle's shape. Based on his ten years of being a therapist at the Halpern Center for Addiction, he was convinced its overall contour and diameter were essential for promoting group interaction.

Ben hurried to his office and tossed the newest edition of the Journal of Solution-Focused Practices into his briefcase. There were a couple of articles he wanted to read over the weekend.

When he arrived home, he decided to wait outside in the driveway, knowing his ten-year-old learning-disabled son, Sam, would be dropped off shortly. He leaned against the car fender, enjoying the warmth of the sun on his face and the gentle southerly breeze ruffling his hair. The smell of freshly mown grass filled his nostrils, and he breathed it in.

Fifteen minutes later, the big yellow bus rounded the bend. The joy on his son's face when he bounded down the bus steps made waiting for him worth it. Father and son linked arms and went inside the house together.

"How was your day?" Ben asked toward Sam's back as the boy flew up the stairs to his bedroom where his video games waited.

"Good, Dad!" Sam yelled.

Ben shook his head. Sam never spoke in a normal tone, but always decibel levels above everybody else's. Ben didn't care. He loved Sam dearly.

Ben tossed his briefcase onto the kitchen counter. A familiar stab of pain struck deep inside when he instinctively looked around for Melinda, as he still sometimes did. Up until eighteen months ago, his wife had always been busy preparing dinner when he arrived home from work. Then came the diagnosis of stage-four breast cancer after what was supposed to be a routine mammogram. The cancer took her from him only months later.

It happened so fast, and she was gone so quickly.

Ben took a deep breath. He missed her every day. The hole she had left in his heart was a gaping, everlasting wound.

After the first six months or so, his friends often told him he should go out more. "Get a life," they said. "Don't cling to the past. Start dating." He wasn't sure letting go of the past would make him feel any better. He wasn't sure he wanted to let go.

He wasn't sure he could.

CHAPTER FIVE

On Monday morning at work, the skreek skreek from Cassie's chair as she rocked back and forth wrecked her concentration. Her memories of Saturday night and Jon's catching her in the lie about being at Sally's didn't help any, either. She'd mumbled a story, something about a night out with the girls and not wanting him to know. Another lie.

It had been late, and fortunately, Jon hadn't pressed her. But the tone of his voice told her he didn't believe her. And then Sunday, she checked her online bank account and discovered she had used up four hundred and ninety dollars of her five hundred in overdraft protection. The little emotional well-being she'd gained back vanished in a plume of remorse.

Still swaying enough to make her chair screech, she forced herself not to dwell on negative thoughts. She managed to work productively for an hour until Wumi stopped by her desk.

"Just dropping by to say hi. How are you, Cass?"

"Not bad. How 'bout you? How was your weekend?" She leaned back from her computer, and her chair screeched enough to make Wumi laugh. Cassie grimaced.

"My weekend was just the usual," Wumi said, still chuckling. "Cleaning, laundry, grocery shopping. Domestic engineering."

"No hot dates?" She'd heard through the office grapevine Wumi was on the lookout for a suitable partner.

"'Fraid not."

"Don't worry, Wumi. He's out there somewhere."

"Maybe." Wumi looked at her watch. "Got to get going. Later." She headed in the direction of her cubicle.

Cassie watched her go, thankful for her own husband and children. Even though they made life more complicated, she couldn't imagine living alone.

She stayed focused on her work, and at the end of the day, she felt she'd been productive. The television squawked from the family room as she arrived home and dropped her purse on the kitchen counter.

"Hi, tribe," she called. "How was your day?" She passed a trail of shoes, backpacks, and jackets in the hall on the way to the family room, where she sat down on the ottoman next to the couch. Anne-Marie and Jesse sprawled over the couch cushions, their eyes glued to the television screen.

"Mine was good," Anne-Marie finally stated, glancing at her mother and then back at the screen. "I got an A on my reading comprehension test."

"Great!" Cassie blew Anne-Marie a kiss. "How 'bout you, Jess?"

"Not so bad. The teacher said I'm doing better in my spelling."

Cassie rose from the ottoman and gave the younger girl a peck on her cheek. "'Atta girl. I knew you could do it!"

A big smile lit up Jesse's face. "Thanks, Mom."

Anne-Marie bounced on the couch to face her. "Hey, Mom, now that it's August, the community center has opened up ice skating. Can we all go tonight? I saw on the digital board outside the center it only costs two dollars a person."

"We'll ask Dad when he comes home, and if he's up for it, it sounds good to me."

HOPE DOESN'T DISAPPOINT

"You wanna go, don't you, Jess?" Anne-Marie eyed her sister hopefully.

"Not really. It's so crowded. We can't practice any of our stuff."

Cassie had been taking the girls for figure skating lessons on Wednesday evenings for the past two years. She took pride in their athletic ability, and she loved watching them practice their routines in preparation for the annual spring skating club extravaganza.

"Aw, c'mon, Jess. It'll be fun. Maybe Mom and Dad will take us for cinnamon waffles and hot chocolate afterwards."

At the mention of food, Jesse perked up. "Oh, all right. I'll go."

Anne-Marie gave her sister a high-five. "Good! Now, we just have to convince Dad."

Jon arrived home from work looking tired but happy.

"Did your team sell lots of cars today?" Cassie greeted him with a hug and kiss.

Jon grinned. "Best day so far this month, and the month's only half over."

"Way to go."

"Can we go to the family ice skating tonight at the community center, Dad? Mom said it's okay with her." Anne-Marie's eyes shone with anticipation.

Jon winked at Cassie. "Sure, why not? And because I had such a good day, I'll take the three of you out for dinner before we go skating. The big question is, where will we go?" They all voted for Italian.

The unanimity of the vote was a minor miracle.

Later, as Cassie and Jon skated arm-in-arm around the rink, she looked up at him. "I'm proud of you. You work so hard to be a success at what you do."

"Well, thank you. And I'm proud of you. Jon looked down at Cassie and his eyes sparkled.

Cassie felt her cheeks redden. Her behavior in the past while hadn't given Jon much to be proud of. She pursed her lips and determined that in the future, she really would do better.

Despite her vow to alter her ways, Cassie couldn't stay away. On Saturday afternoon, as she walked into the casino after Jon had taken the girls for their piano lessons, the atmosphere encircled her like a mother's embrace. Not that she knew much about such things. As a child, her mother had seldom shown her physical affection, except sometimes when she was sober. The hugs she received then were special.

"Are you all right?"

Startled, she stared at a female attendant who regarded her with concern.

Blushing, Cassie realized she had been standing still, staring off into space.

"I—uh, I'm fine. I guess I was woolgathering."

"Would you like a drink of water?"

"No, really, I'm fine. But thanks."

The woman smiled and walked away.

Cassie strode briskly to one of the machines, embarrassed by the encounter. As soon as the multi-colored images started whizzing by, she relaxed, entering the zone where nothing else existed except the moving symbols and the anticipation of a big win.

Although she didn't collect a jackpot, Cassie mustered all her willpower and forced herself to leave before it got to be too late. She didn't want to give Jon any reason to suspect her. However, as she headed to the exit, she couldn't resist looking back at the patrons, wishing she could still be playing.

Later that night, as Cassie sat in front of her computer in her home office, the glare from the monitor—or was it the numbers?—hurt her eyes as she stared at her online bank statements. She was way over her credit protection limit. Ms. Doyle would be calling her soon for another heart-to-heart chat.

How could she rectify the situation? She desperately needed money to cover the overdraft. Her brain was shifting into overdrive, searching for a solution, when her eyes fell on her expense reports from Bigelows. She'd brought them home to work on, since they were due Monday. She picked up the reports and examined them.

All it will take is a little tweak here and there. Lorna will never notice it.

CHAPTER SIX

Fall arrived in the city of Kettering. The leaves on the trees changed color and the days grew shorter. The shimmering summer blue water of Lake Ontario turned to gray as autumn's crispness permeated the air. Although the days were shorter, people spent as much time outside as possible, knowing winter would come too soon.

After stacking their dinner's last dish in the dishwasher, Cassie stuck her head out her back door. The fresh breeze tantalized her.

"I'm going for a stroll," she called, and the girls came running.

"Can we come with you?"

"Of course. I'd love some company."

At that moment, Jon also appeared at the back door. Jesse grabbed his hand and smiled up at him.

"Come with us for a walk, Dad. You need more exercise. I don't think you get enough." Jon reached down and tousled her hair.

The sun was beginning to set, painting tinges of pink, orange, and violet across the western sky. People were out walking their dogs, and Cassie and Jon greeted them as they passed.

Their stroll eventually took them into one of the town's older sections, with homes dating back to the late nineteen forties. They were smaller, set closer to the sidewalk, and the space between houses was narrower.

Just as they turned to start back, loud shouts from a house across the street echoed down the pavement. They slowed their steps, partly from surprise and partly from curiosity.

"I can't believe you lost your job again." The female voice was a sawmill blade of sound, a screech of ripping pine board. "If you laid off the sauce, maybe you wouldn't keep getting fired from work."

A male voice spoke lower, gruffer, harder to hear. "You're one to talk. When's the last time you worked?"

"Hard to work when you have three little kids and no one to take care of 'em."

"I'll take care of 'em," the male voice answered. "You go get a job."

"Yeah, right," the female retorted. "The minute I leave for work, you'll be off at Jonny's Bar and Grill, leaving the kids to fend for themselves." Footsteps pounded up a stairwell, followed by the boom of a forcibly closed door.

Jon and the girls continued to walk. Cassie didn't move. After a few moments, Jon returned to her, with the children behind him.

"What's the matter, Mom?" Anne-Marie asked.

Cassie massaged her temples. "Nothing for you to worry about, sweetheart. It just upsets me when I hear people fighting."

"Me too." Jesse's eyes were wide.

"It distresses most people." Jon took Cassie's hand, and they began walking again. Anne-Marie and Jesse, after another look at their mother, skipped ahead.

"Unpleasant memories?" he asked.

Seconds passed before she answered.

"That fighting made me feel like a little girl again, lying in my bed, listening to my parents brawl in the next room. I remember my dad always ragging at my mom when he got home from work—the house was a pigsty, I was all alone, she was nowhere to be found—on and on and on."

"Your childhood sure wasn't the greatest."

"The bickering never stopped, and Mom never quit drinking." Cassie stood perfectly still, staring into the distance. Another long moment went by before she turned and looked at Jon. "It finally killed her. She was only forty-two. Not that much older than I am now." A tear edged down one cheek, and she swiped it away with her finger.

"Such a waste." Jon gave Cassie's hand a squeeze as they gazed into the night sky and watched as it filled with twinkling stars. Cassie pointed out the Big Dipper, and Jon found Orion.

"My dad was never the same after Mom's death. For some reason, we were never able to share our grief or comfort each other. Even though there were two of us in the house, I felt so lonely."

Anne-Marie and Jesse had run far ahead, and Jon called for them to slow down.

"And then I met you," she said, "just before our senior year in high school. That was a godsend."

Jon bent down and kissed her on the head. "Our senior year of high school and the years at McMaster University were good ones, weren't they?"

Cassie nodded.

When they reached their house, Jon stopped in front of the walkway and turned to her. "You know, after all you went through as a child, some counseling might be helpful for you. What do you think?"

"No, Jon, I'm good. That argument we heard just took me back. That's all."

CHAPTER SEVEN

On Monday evening, Cassie sat in the family room, closed her eyes, and leaned her head back against the couch. Jon would be home from work extra late and Anne-Marie and Jesse were upstairs playing a game on their computer. Nodding off, she jerked awake when a car on the street misfired. She checked her watch. By now, the girls should be in bed reading. Time to go up and kiss them goodnight.

Anne-Marie lay on her bed, her nose stuck in a book. She barely glanced up when her mother walked into her bedroom. "Lights out, sweetie."

"Just let me finish this chapter, and then, I promise I'll turn them off."

Cassie hesitated. It wouldn't hurt if her daughter stayed up an extra ten minutes or so. Anne-Marie looked at her with pleading eyes. "Please?"

Cassie bent down and gave her a kiss. "Okay. But if you're tired tomorrow morning, I'll know you didn't keep your promise."

"I'll keep it, Mom."

She blew her daughter a kiss before walking out the door

Jesse's room was dark. As her eyes adjusted to the dimness, she saw Jesse lying on her bed, her face toward the wall.

"I came in to kiss you goodnight, honey." She switched on the light and walked closer to the bed. "Are you all right?"

Jesse didn't answer and Cassie thought she heard a hiccup. "What's the matter?" She sat down on the side of the bed and stroked her daughter's back. "Did something happen at school today?"

What happened? Jesse had been in good spirits at dinner. "Tell me, sweetheart. I don't like to see you upset."

Slowly, Jesse rolled over and Cassie could see she'd been crying. She pulled her daughter to a sitting position and held her in her arms. "What is it?"

Jesse sobbed. "Sarah called me stupid."

"When?"

"Just now."

"What do you mean?"

"She sent me a text with one word on it. It said 'stupid'."

"Why would she do that?"

'Cause I'm slower in arithmetic than she is."

"That's no reason to call you stupid. We all learn at different rates."

Jesse's sobs had let up, but she began again in earnest. "And she's not the only one. Sometimes the other girls don't want to play with me because they say I'm too slow."

"Slow at what?"

"I don't run into the skipping rope fast enough."

"That's no reason not to play with you."

"When I walk over to play, a girl named Tanya pushes me away."

Cassie had seen Tanya. She was a heavy-set girl a good two inches taller than Jesse.

"Do I need to talk to your teacher about this?"

"N-o-o-o," Jesse wailed. Anxiety filled her eyes. "He'll just say we need to learn to work things out ourselves."

HOPE DOESN'T DISAPPOINT

"But if someone's physically pushing you, that's bullying. Something needs to be done about it."

Memories from her own school days jumbled around in her head like marbles hitting against each other, making her heart pound and her hands sweaty. If she lived to be a hundred, she'd never forget the jeers she got at school.

"Doesn't your mother wash your clothes? You're smelly."

"There's a hole in the toe of your shoe."

"Peanut butter breath. All you ever have are peanut butter sandwiches."

As she sat on the bed beside Jesse, Cassie's eyes filled with tears. Often the only thing in the house was peanut butter and some stale bread, if her mom had been too drunk to go to the store. She cleared her throat and swore to herself her child would not suffer what she'd suffered.

"Bullies have to be stopped. We can't let this continue."

"P-l-e-a-s-e don't do anything, Mom. I'll find some new friends."

She decided not to upset Jesse any further. She'd bring the matter up at the next teacher interview. "Lie down, sweetie. It's getting late."

"Promise you won't do anything, Mom?"

"We'll talk about it tomorrow. Right now you need to get to sleep."

Jesse rubbed her eyes before snuggling under the covers. "Please don't ..." Her eyes closed. "Please don't ..." Within seconds, her even breathing told Cassie she had fallen asleep. She stood and kissed her on the forehead.

Back in the family room, Cassie paced up and down the floor, her stomach in jitters. Anxiety about her daughter being bullied and memories of her own school days threatened to overwhelm her.

Her fingers twitched, needing to punch buttons and trigger the lights and sounds.

Go to the casino.

Today was Monday. She wouldn't be able to get there until Saturday. She didn't know if she could wait that long.

Saturday.

CHAPTER EIGHT

Cassie looked at her cell phone and nearly collapsed.
10 a.m., Sunday, November 5.
Sunday? The day couldn't be right. The room spun around her. She felt faint, near passing out. Trembling, she hurried over to the well-dressed woman at the next machine. The sickly-sweet odor of her perfume added to Cassie's light-headedness.

"What's the date today?"

Ignoring her, the woman continued to play the machine.

Cassie watched in disbelief. "Would you please check your cell phone for me? It's important."

Frowning, the woman reached for her purse and pulled out her phone. "It's Sunday the fifth," she growled, eyeing Cassie as if she wasn't quite right in the head. "Seven minutes after ten in the morning."

All night. I've stayed all night.

Cassie hurried back to her machine and picked up her purse. Even though she'd won a jackpot, nearly all her winnings were gone.

She strode across the carpet to the exit. Jon would be worried sick. Maybe he'd even called the police. And what would the girls think when they learned their mother had stayed out all night?

In the parking lot, she fumbled with the car keys, dropped them, swore softly, and finally got the car door open. Once inside, she sat and stared out the windshield, her heart hammering, anxiety boiling in her stomach. She shoved the car door open and raced to a nearby grassy area where she bent almost double dry heaving. When the spasms stopped, she swabbed the back of her hand across her mouth and lurched back to her car.

Cassie leaned against the driver's door of the Honda and slowly slid to the ground. She couldn't tell Jon she'd been out with the girls all night. Her body shook with sobs. What was she going to do?

Her telephone signaled a text message. She yanked the phone from her pocket.

JON: Where are u? Please, please Cassie, text me and let me know u r ok

She looked at her call history. Jon had called and texted her most of the night. For all those hours, the slot machine in front of her had erased everything and everyone else.

Cassie texted back.

CASSIE: I'm okay. B right home

She pushed herself up and off the pavement and got into her car. Her hands rebelled as she fumbled to start the engine. She skidded out of the parking lot, her tires squealing as she turned into the street.

Silence greeted Cassie when she walked through her front door.

"Is anybody home?"

Jon emerged from the family room, disheveled, dark circles under his eyes.

Cassie set down her purse and keys in the hallway. "Where are the girls?"

"I took them over to my mom's. They didn't want to go." He took a deep breath. "I told them when they got back, you'd be home."

There was a long moment of cold, empty silence. She covered her face with her hands. "I'm so sorry, Jon."

"I was about to call the police when you texted me back." He strode to the couch in the family room and motioned her to sit beside him. "What's going on?" He searched her face. "Are you seeing someone else?"

"Of course not." Her voice sounded angry, even to her own ears. She reached for his hand and squeezed it. His fingers were ice.

"Where were you?"

Cassie bowed her head and stared at the floor rather than looking him in the eye. "I was at the casino. I lost track of time."

"Is that where you were when you gave me that cock-and-bull story about being out with the girls?"

She nodded.

"Are you addicted or something?"

"I'm fine. I just like the slot machines. It's entertainment."

Skepticism was written all over Jon's face as he stared at her.

"Well, your entertainment sure caused a lot of grief in this family last night."

"I won't go anymore." She touched Jon's hand again, and found it a little warmer. "I promise."

"Don't do it again, Cass." His look was one of disapproval, same as the glares her father had given her when she came home way past her curfew.

"I won't." She stared past his shoulder at the wall.

He cleared his throat. "We'd better get in touch with my mom and let everyone know you're home safe." He stood. "I'll call."

Cassie rose hastily from the couch.

"I'll do it." She pulled her cell phone from her pocket and walked into the kitchen. She didn't want the girls or her in-laws to hear the story from Jon. As she stared at the screen, her brain went into overdrive, trying to figure out how she could spin things in the best possible light.

CHAPTER NINE

Cassie's boss Lorna cornered her early on a snowy Thursday afternoon.

"I'd like you to go to a five-day trade show just outside Chicago, starting this coming Monday."

Cassie grimaced. "That's going to take a lot of juggling for me at home. Why didn't you tell me about it last week?"

"I apologize for that. I just learned about it today. It's a brand-new exhibition, and I think it's important for Bigelows to be represented."

"Can't Wumi go?'

"She's heading out west to check out a new vendor."

"You really think it's important for someone from Bigelows to be there?"

"I do."

Cassie sighed. "Provided I can get everything organized, I'll go."

"That sounds fair."

Cassie managed to get things sorted out before she had to leave. Flying out of Ottawa's Macdonald-Cartier International Airport early on Monday morning, she landed at Chicago's O'Hare, where she hired a cab to take her to her hotel in St. Charles.

St. Charles, around thirty-nine miles west of Chicago, didn't appear to be very big. To give it credit, she did pass the picturesque Fox River, quite a few nice parks, and a good-sized museum. The quaint city center looked pristine in its blanket of fluffy white snow.

The cab deposited her at a boutique hotel, its charcoal-gray concrete façade rising eight stories above the landscape. Cassie hoped it had a swimming pool. She felt a sudden inclination to plunge into some warm water.

Her room was an end unit on the eighth floor with a panoramic view of the area. Throwing her suitcase and hand luggage onto the bed, she picked up one of the hotel's amenities folders from the coffee table. There was indeed a pool on the fifth floor that stayed open until eleven in the evening, which meant she could get in a swim when she got back from the trade show each day.

About to toss the folder aside, Cassie noticed the hotel had a casino. She quickly put the folder back as if she had touched something hot, remembering her promise to Jon she wouldn't gamble.

The next day, Cassie left the trade show floor depressed and tired, unimpressed with the goods she had seen. She had made one buy, but apart from that she didn't have anything else to show for a whole day of traipsing around and talking to vendors.

That evening she hit the pool. Large, with glass windows all around, it was equipped with numerous lounge chairs and a sizable spa. Very few patrons were using the facility, and Cassie had it nearly all to herself. She spent twenty minutes swimming laps, and the water soothed away the stress of the day.

The next day, the show's organizers had brought in new merchandise, and more vendors had set up shop. She visited each one and arranged three more purchases for a total of four buys. Not a great result for a Chicago show.

When she returned to the hotel, she took out her cell phone and called Lorna.

"Hello, Bigelows, Lorna Nelson speaking. How can I help you?"

"Hi, Lorna. It's Cassie."

"How's the trade show? Lots of trend-setting stuff?"

"No way. Somebody in their advertising department bent the truth quite a bit. I've looked at everything—and I mean everything—and I've only made four buys. I don't think it makes much sense for me to stay until the end of the week, so I'd like to arrange an earlier flight and come home."

Several seconds passed before Lorna spoke. "Well, you never know, they may bring in more inventory. I'd really like you to stay until the end."

Cassie sighed. "Is that an order?"

"Not an order. A request from your boss."

"You're not making this easy. I'll stay, but I think the company is wasting its money keeping me here."

"I hear you, Cass. See you when you get back."

Cassie ended the call with Lorna and called home. She enjoyed hearing the girls' voices, learning that Jon's days had been busy and productive, and that Nellie was holding her own.

When she hung up, familiar feelings of loneliness and isolation set in, bringing with them restlessness. She paced up and down the length of the room, but the small space only increased her agitation. A stroll around the hotel might be just the cure.

In the elevator, the advertisement for the casino flashed at Cassie like a neon sign, and the lure of winning a jackpot pulled her like a magnet.

Jon will never find out.

She headed for the casino and the slot machines. She sat, pressed the button, and slowly her edginess lessened.

At four the next morning, Cassie climbed into her hotel bed. She set the alarm for seven o'clock, hoping she'd be able to get up.

A dream of being buried in a mound of coins filled her mind. She kept trying to climb out, but her limbs seemed paralyzed. As she pushed with all her might, a bee buzzed loudly around her head. Startled, she opened her eyes and realized the bee was the alarm clock.

"Shut up," she groaned, straining to find the snooze button.

When Cassie woke up next, she stared at the clock radio beside the bed. Four p.m. She had slept through all the snooze alarms.

In a panic, she hopped out of bed and headed to the bathroom. She'd gotten into the shower and was rinsing her hair when it hit her that the trade show closed at six o'clock. She wasn't going to make it in time.

Leaning her head against the bathroom wall, she groaned. She'd messed things up royally. But the hot shower lifted her spirits, and a half hour later she set out for the casino with renewed hope.

The next day she didn't climb out of bed until four-thirty in the afternoon, missing a second day of the show. The adage 'the definition of insanity is repeating the same behavior over and over and expecting different results' had run through Cassie's brain more than once during the evening. Whenever it did, she'd shove the thought away and keep playing.

Knowing the trade show was already a bust, she spent the next day and a half at the casino. As she headed for home on Friday afternoon, a heaviness settled over her, like a weighty hand crushing her. She'd only made four show buys, far worse than she'd ever done as a junior buyer. To add insult to injury, she hadn't won a jackpot at the casino.

She didn't even want to think about how much money she'd lost. Her mind flew in a million different directions as she scrambled for an explanation for Lorna.

Monday morning, Cassie sat in Lorna's office, her eyes fixed on her supervisor's hands on the desk.

"What's going on, Cassie? Even when you first started, you purchased more merchandise than this."

"I told you. It was a lousy show." Cassie wrapped her sweater around her, chilled from more than just the weather.

Lorna stared at the piece of paper in front of her.

"I have a friend who attended the show." Her voice sounded strained. "She said she only saw someone from Bigelows for the first two days. What did you do the rest of the time?"

"I—um—I took three days of vacation."

Lorna's gaze was intense. "Vacation? You know vacation requires approval. And it's not right to take vacation when you're on a paid business trip."

"You sent me on a goose chase that wasted my time and kept me from buying better products somewhere else. That was just—just wrong." Cassie glared defiantly at Lorna.

Lorna tapped her pen on her desktop. "You and I have been colleagues for a long time, and I hate to do this, but you leave me no choice. I'm going to make a note in your personnel file about the poor results from the trade show, and the fact you took unauthorized vacation on a business trip."

Heat rose in Cassie's cheeks. "Do what you have to do." She stood. "I'll do better next time."

"I hope so." Lorna's penetrating gaze made Cassie's face even hotter.

Back at her workstation, she yanked out her chair and plopped down with a thud. In her mind, she plotted how she would find a job with one of Bigelows' competitors and give another company her years of experience. Then Bigelows would be sorry. They'd learn they couldn't mess with her.

CHAPTER TEN

On Wednesday night, two days after Cassie's confrontation with Lorna, she sat idly at the computer in her home office playing solitaire. Everyone else had gone to bed, but she'd been unable to sleep.

An hour passed before she felt tired enough to return to bed. She was just about to shut off the computer when a pop-up ad for online fantasy poker flashed onto the screen. Memories of playing free online poker in college—and being good at it—came to mind. She stared at the ad for several seconds, wondering if her previous skill would still work for her. Clicking onto the site, she entered her information and table name and was assigned one thousand fantasy dollars to start.

Cassie played for an hour, pleased to find she could hold her own. When her vision started to blur, she switched off her computer and tiptoed back to the bedroom. Muffled snores came from Jon, who had half his face buried in the pillow. Slipping quietly into the bed, she snuggled close to him and wrapped her arm around his waist. Jon rolled onto his side. Within minutes, his snoring resumed.

Several evenings passed before Cassie had an opportunity to return to the online fantasy poker site. Her last time at the casino she had lost nine hundred dollars, but won a thousand-dollar jackpot, giving her a net gain of one hundred dollars. She decided to use the hundred to see how well she did online when she played for real money.

Credit card in hand, determined to play conservatively, Cassie ran her hundred dollars up to three hundred and twenty in winnings in the space of an hour. The next game she played, she went all in and lost, and pushed herself away from the computer. She stayed awake a long time afterward, thinking through what she could have done differently.

"Morning, Mom." Jesse stared at her over the breakfast table the next day. "You look like a raccoon. You've got dark circles around your eyes. You sleep okay?"

Cassie blinked and stared at her daughter. "I look that bad?"

Jesse nodded.

"I guess I'll have to use extra makeup today."

"A floppy hat that covers your eyes might be good."

Cassie couldn't help laughing. "I'll add some sunglasses to complete the look."

Jesse gave her mother a bear hug. "I love you, Mom."

"Love you, too." Cassie nuzzled her nose in her daughter's sweet-smelling hair. "Now get ready for school."

When Cassie arrived home from work that evening, Anne-Marie and Jesse rushed her at the front door, both shouting at the same time.

"Mom, Mom! We've been invited to a sleepover this Saturday for Aubrey's birthday party. Can we go?"

Cassie took off her coat and hung it up. "Aubrey Kettleby from down the street?"

Both girls frowned.

"Of course, Mom," Anne-Marie said. "Who else would it be?"

"Just checking. I'll speak to Aubrey's mom to confirm things."

"Can you call right now?" Jesse pleaded. "We want to know if we can go."

Cassie frowned at her daughter. "I'll call after dinner. Now please go set the table."

Jesse stomped off to the kitchen, Anne-Marie on her heels.

"And don't forget to empty the dishwasher and put the dishes away. That was supposed to be done when you got home from school."

"Aw, Mom, we were too tired when we got home."

"And maybe I'm too tired to call Aubrey's mother about the sleepover."

Cupboard doors banged and cutlery clinked. The possibility of not being able to go to the sleepover had lit a firecracker under the girls' bottoms. Cassie couldn't help smiling.

After the girls had gone to bed that night, Jon and Cassie sat side-by-side in their room, propped on pillows against the headboard. Jon's laptop was open in front of him as he analyzed his team's car sales for the month. Cassie aimlessly flipped through a book she found less than inspiring.

"I forgot to tell you," Jon said. "The dealership has asked me to participate in an online lead generation webinar this weekend. I can do it from here, but it means I'll be tied up on Saturday from one to five o'clock."

"Hmm." Cassie looked up from her paperback and realized she'd read the same sentence three times. "I've cancelled the girls' piano lessons for this week because they have their sleepover on Saturday for Aubrey Kettleby's birthday."

Jon's face asked the question, *Who's Aubrey Kettleby?*

"They're our neighbors down the street."

"Oh, that Aubrey. The mouthy one?"

Cassie laughed. "Let's just say she's opinionated." She closed her book and put it on the night table. "I'll have to buy a birthday present for her before Saturday."

"Do you have any other plans for Saturday?"

Cassie grimaced. "Just the usual. Dusting, vacuuming, laundry, and fitting in the grocery shopping."

"I'll do the grocery shopping," Jon volunteered. "I'll even help with the vacuuming. We'll get everything done in the morning, so you'll have Saturday afternoon to yourself."

Leaning over, Cassie planted a lingering kiss on Jon's mouth. "Now I know why I married you."

Jon laid his laptop on the floor and scooted closer to Cassie. "Was that an invitation?" He smoothed a loose strand of hair behind her ear.

"It could be."

Afterwards she whispered, "I love you, Jonathan Bailey."

"I love you, too, Cassandra Bailey."

By three o'clock Saturday afternoon, Cassie had folded the last of the laundry and put it away. She looked around from the couch in the family room where she'd landed for a break. The house was quiet and unusually still, with the girls at the sleepover and Jon closed in the office for his webinar. She wandered into the kitchen, picked up her laptop, and brought it into the family room. The money she'd lost at the online poker session had been niggling at her, and she couldn't shake the notion she'd allowed the game to best her. Determined to win the money back, she typed in the web address for the site.

Over the course of the first few hands, Cassie almost recouped the blown money. Then she took a chance on a pot, went all in, and lost. The loss infuriated her, steeling her resolve to get her money back.

Two hours later, Cassie had lost two thousand dollars, all of it charged to her credit card. She was about to start another game when Jon's footsteps sounded on the stairs. She shut off her computer and took it into the kitchen. Then she sprinted back to the family room, flopped onto the couch, snatched up a random magazine from the coffee table, and ruffled through the pages as he came in.

"How was your webinar?"

"Just what I expected." Jon sat down on the couch and looked closely at Cassie. "You sound out of breath and your face is pale. Are you okay?"

"I'm fine." Cassie's eyes veered off to the side. Jon stared at her, not speaking. She shrugged. "Maybe I'm coming down with a cold or something."

"Let's hope not."

Cassie hated herself for doing it. Night after night, she returned to the online gambling site. On weekends whenever Jon and the girls were occupied elsewhere, she sat down with her laptop in the most private place she could find, desperate to win back her losses.

Weeks went by. Cassie kept playing. A month passed before she maxed out her credit cards and accessed the bank line of credit she and Jon shared. Frantic, far beyond the point of weighing the risks and rewards of her actions, Cassie kept chasing her losses.

Alone at the kitchen island late one Friday night, she stared at their online bank statements. According to the bank's credit report, she'd tapped their line of credit for almost one hundred thousand dollars. She struggled to breathe. She covered her face with her hands and listened to the wailing inside her head.

I've got to stop. I have to stop!

Unable to sleep most nights due to either gambling online or worrying about it, Cassie had problems functioning at work. On a couple of occasions, Lorna asked if she was okay. The third time her boss came to her was to point out irregularities on the last few expense reports Cassie had submitted.

"How can that be?" Cassie did her Hollywood best to look surprised, then reached out and snatched the reports from Lorna's hand. "I'll straighten it out," she said curtly, hating the look on Lorna's face.

But the session with Lorna was nothing compared to the night Jon stormed into the kitchen with their bank statements. Anger poured off him like cold smoke off ice as he thumped down onto the tableside chair next to her. His voice was barely above a growl.

"What is all this about? This? And this?"

He jabbed his finger again and again at the printout on the table. The paper was creased and bent where the amount owed on their line of credit was printed.

"Stop it, Jon," she pleaded, rubbing her temples. "Pounding on the table is giving me a headache." When he didn't respond, she sat upright and made a calm down gesture with her hand. "I can explain."

"Be my guest," Jon barked.

She breathed deep. This was not going to be easy.

"To relax at night, I've been playing online poker. There've been times when I was ahead. Now I'm behind."

"Yeah. One hundred thousand dollars behind, to be exact."

Cassie began to cry.

"Do you realize—no, do you even care that this house we're sitting in serves as collateral for the line of credit?" he asked, his voice a scant decibel lower. "It was only to be used in case of an emergency, like losing our jobs or something like that."

Jon shook his head and his eyes glinted like daggers. "You know our budget. It takes both our salaries to make the mortgage payment and pay the bills, with nothing left over at the end of the month. It's not like we have savings hidden away somewhere." He picked up the bank statement and slapped it down on the table. "I don't know how we're going to pay this back."

Cassie fought the fog in her brain, scrambling to find a solution. "I'll cut back on my expenses and pay a certain amount off each month."

Jon scoffed. "Even if you paid off one thousand dollars every month, which is highly unlikely, it would take you over eight years to pay off everything. And that's without any interest being added each month."

"Shh," Cassie begged. "You'll wake the girls."

He waved his arm in the air in a dismissive gesture. "How considerate of you not to want to wake them. Nice." He brought his face close to hers, anger written in its lines and creases. "Did you think about them when you were gambling away money we don't have?" Jon took a deep breath and his shoulders slumped. "We should be putting money away for their education, not blowing it away—in fact, we should have started a long time ago. Now—" He shrugged helplessly. "—now we won't be able to."

Neither of them spoke for several minutes, each lost in thought, until he spoke again.

"Get your credit cards." His voice was unexpectedly harsh.

When she returned, credit cards in hand, Jon took a pair of kitchen shears out of the drawer and cut them up. "Cancel the accounts."

She covered her face with her hands, not wanting him to know the rest of the bad news. He stared at her in silence for a moment before he spoke.

"Are they maxed out?" He pulled one of her hands down. "Look at me!"

She looked into his eyes, into the anger and pain in his face.

"You maxed them out, didn't you?"

She sat silent, not willing to admit the truth.

"Maxed," he said, his voice edged in stone. "With interest rates of over nineteen percent on each card." Jon swept his arm over the table, raking the credit card bits onto the floor.

The silence weighed heavily as they stared everywhere but at each other.

"You've got to get professional help, Cassie. This is not entertainment. This is a life-altering addiction." His voice fractured on the last three words.

Sobs shook her.

"I'm sorry, Jon, so sorry." She wrung her hands. "I'll stop gambling. I'll go for counseling."

He gave her a look that said *yeah, right, like before when you said you'd stop gambling*.

"I promise, Jon. Don't you believe me?"

His look grew even more skeptical.

"This time I'll keep my promise." Through sheer determination, she maintained eye contact with him. Relief flooded her when he looked away. "I promise."

CHAPTER ELEVEN

The week's group session for addicted gamblers had ended. Ben sat in his office, looking out the window at the snow. The groundhog had seen its shadow. Six more weeks of winter. Sometimes the dreariness weighed him down, especially after hearing the group members' stories. The one that got to him most was Frank's. He had lost his wife and children due to his gambling, and it wasn't until shady loan shark enforcers beat him senseless that he realized the gravity of his situation.

Ben shook his head. How sad an addiction could take someone so deep. Deciding he didn't want the sagas of his group members to pull him down, Ben stood up, grabbed his briefcase, and left the office.

As he headed home, a knot of nerves formed in his stomach, centering on Maddie O'Reilly. The previous Sunday after church service, when everyone was out in the foyer having coffee and snacks, Ben found her standing near and smiling up at him. Her dark curls, cobalt blue eyes, and million-dollar grin flummoxed him.

Maddie, a nurse, worked in a husband-and-wife pediatricians' office. Two and a half years earlier, she'd lost her husband, Tom, to prostate cancer. The cancer had metastasized to his pelvis, leading to incapacitating pain and a difficult death. When Ben's wife Melinda was taken from him by her cancer, Maddie had dropped off meals for Ben and Sam on behalf of the church.

As Ben and Maddie talked over the church snacks and coffee, he realized they had a lot in common. When someone flicked the lights to indicate the church doors were closing, they looked at each other in surprise. "Is it that time already?" Maddie asked. "I'd better track down the twins." The twins were her identical twin girls, a couple of years older than Sam.

"And who knows where Sam is?" Chagrined, Ben realized he'd forgotten about his son. He turned to look for Sam, then on impulse turned back to Maddie.

"I've really enjoyed our chat. Would you like to meet for coffee at the donut shop around the corner? Say maybe next Friday, around seven-thirty?"

Seconds passed before Maddie answered, and Ben felt like a high school freshman who had just asked a girl out for his first date.

"I'd love to."

Had he heard right? He had. He couldn't stop grinning.

Now Friday had arrived. He had to rush home before Sam got home from school, take him over to his grandma's house for the night, and get ready to meet Maddie at seven-thirty.

Dear Lord Jesus, I invite you to come with Maddie and me tonight, he prayed silently as he drove. *Both of us have lost our spouses. I know I'm lonely, and I suspect Maddie is too. Thank you for loving us, and for guiding us in the good path you've laid out for us to follow.*

CHAPTER TWELVE

Cassie grew more secretive in her gambling and more adept at lying to Jon, after she broke her promise to stop gambling and go for counseling. He'd blocked her access to the line of credit and their joint bank account, but she still gambled. The thrill was too good to give up.

But the thrill couldn't make up for the day Jon came into the kitchen holding an official-looking letter, his face sallow, his shoulders drooped in defeat.

"Your lies have brought us to this." He tossed the document down on the counter in front of her.

She picked up the document and scanned it quickly. Her heart thudded, and pain threatened to burst through her temples. "Isn't there anything we can do?"

He shook his head. "I spoke with the bank. Unless we can pay off that one hundred-thousand-dollar line of credit by the end of this month, the bank will take this house."

An inner fire of panic and shame burned Cassie's cheeks. "There has to be something we can do."

"I've explored every resource I know of. Nothing has worked out."

Cassie sank down on a padded stool at the kitchen island, put her arms on the counter, and buried her face in her arms.

Minutes passed before Jon spoke again, his voice barely above a whisper.

"I love you, and I always will. That's why it breaks my heart to say this." He took a deep breath. "But for the girls' sake, we should separate."

Cassie raised her head and stared blankly at him. "How can our separating help them?"

"Until you admit to yourself you have a problem and truly decide to do something about it, the girls will be better off away from you. After the foreclosure, Anne-Marie and Jesse and I will move back in with my parents. I've already spoken to them."

"What about me?"

Jon shrugged. "I don't know. Maybe you want to think about moving in with your dad."

Her jaw dropped.

"I'd rather live in a gutter than live with my dad!" She slid off the stool and fled from the room.

The bank foreclosed at the end of February. The anguish on the girls' faces as they sat in the car, waiting for their dad to drive them away from the house where they'd lived since they were babies, was etched on her brain forever.

"Mom, come with us," they begged through the open car windows, tears streaming down their faces. "We want you with us."

Cassie had opened the back door of the car, climbed in, and squished down in front of them.

"I have some problems I need to straighten out." Her voice broke and she took their hands, trying hard to compose herself. "It doesn't mean I don't love you." She didn't know if she could finish. "We'll get back together. I promise." Cassie lowered her eyes, unable to look in their sorrowful faces, unsure she'd be able to keep her promise.

In April, after three write-ups in her personnel file for—among other things—failure to show up for work, Lorna terminated her employment. Cassie couldn't believe it was over. She'd started at Bigelows right after her graduation from university and spent twelve years there. And now it was all gone, blown up, the pieces lying in tatters around her feet. And to see the miserable, betrayed look in her boss's eyes the day she told Cassie the news—that had been torture. She knew she'd broken Lorna's heart.

After the foreclosure, Cassie resolved to stay in shelters, remaining in each one until she wore out her welcome. Her first shelter visit changed her mind. After checking in, she was shown to a room with four other beds. Two of her roommates sat on one of them, playing gin rummy. The woman nearest Cassie was heavyset with a shaved head, except for a few long curly tendrils on top. The other was thin as a famine victim, her teeth blackened and crumbling. They eyed Cassie up and down.

"Nice outfit," the heavyset one said. Cassie noticed the thin one was eyeing her purse.

Cassie excused herself quickly and went to the washroom. Sheets of toilet paper and paper towel were strewn all over the floor, despite the oversized garbage can by the door. She cringed when she saw a used menstrual pad hanging over the side of the container. In one corner, a woman sat on the floor, her arm tied up with a tourniquet, mainlining some unknown drug into her vein. Another woman came out of a stall without even looking at the one sitting on the floor. Right then, Cassie decided to leave, knowing she wouldn't be able to sleep in this place. She would live in her car. In her car, at least she had a modicum of control.

Suzanne Graziano tossed her pen onto the desk in the interview room at the precinct jail. She stared at Cassie for several seconds. Then she reached into her purse and pulled out a check book. "How much did you say you owe for the parking tickets?"

"Nine hundred and fifty dollars," Cassie answered, her voice small. She watched as Suzanne began writing out a check. "What are you doing?"

"I'm paying your parking tickets. It's my good deed for the month."

Cassie's eyes widened.

"On one condition," the lawyer said, emphasizing each word with a wave of her pen.

"What's that?"

"You get professional help."

Cassie nodded.

"And believe me, Cassie, I have many contacts. Eyes and ears everywhere. And my fingers are in numerous pies, so to speak. I will know if you're not getting the help you need."

Cassie nodded again.

"I suggest you go to the Halpern Center for Addiction. They have a good reputation."

"All right." Cassie bobbed her head for the third time.

Suzanne stood to leave.

"I don't know how to thank you." Tears filled Cassie's eyes and threatened to spill down her cheeks.

"Just get your head on straight and attend the therapy. You need to stop gambling," Suzanne retorted, and walked out the door.

CHAPTER THIRTEEN

 Late one afternoon, Cassie parked her car in the crowded parking lot and scurried toward Walmart. Her bag of dirty clothes overflowed, and she needed to purchase some laundry detergent and another tube of toothpaste. May had turned out to be a beautiful month with sunshine most days and moderate temperatures, and today, with not a cloud in the sky, she lifted her face to the sun and smiled at its warmth. The delightful weather and fresh spring air helped her to forget about living in her car.
 Inside the store, she pushed her cart along the laundry aisle, searching for the cheapest product available. She'd just dropped some no-name detergent into her buggy when she spotted Nancy Hesser, her old neighbor. She couldn't remember how much she owed the woman, but she knew it was more than a hundred, maybe as much as a hundred and fifty bucks. She peeked around the end of the aisle and watched which way Nancy went, and then she hustled off in the opposite direction. No way did she want to run into the lady.
 Watching as she walked, she hurried to the pharmacy section, where she picked up some toothpaste and a new tooth brush. Her old one had become ratty. On her way to checkout, she ran into Nancy at the end of the pain medication aisle.

"Well, hello, Cassie. I haven't seen you since your family moved away. How are you?"

The woman hadn't changed a bit. Dressed stylishly as always. Cassie could tell she'd just had her blonde hair cut, and it fell in a neat bob around her neck and ears. Heat rose from Cassie's chest to the top of her head as she looked surreptitiously at her own dirty tee shirt, faded blue jeans, and scuffed runners with a hole in one of the toes.

"I'm good. And you?'

"Hubby and the kids are great. Hubby just got a big promotion, and we've been looking at some larger houses on the other side of town. There's a new development going in by the Artisan Group. I'm sure you've heard of them. They design custom homes with all the bells and whistles, and I mean all the bells and whistles. We've been talking with them. The homes aren't cheap, but we think they can design something that will meet our needs."

"How nice." The wheels in Cassie's head ground, making her temples throb, as she tried to figure out how to get away as fast as possible. "I'm in a bit of a hurry." To add emphasis to her words, she made a show of looking at her watch. "Oh my, it's five-thirty. Time for dinner. I've got to go." She pushed her cart.

Nancy ignored Cassie's comments and continued to talk. "I don't know if you heard, but old Mrs. Hutchinson died."

"I'm sorry to hear that."

"You remember the Taylors, the ones who keep their lawn looking like a golf course fairway?" When Cassie didn't respond, Nancy continued. "Well, they took Mrs. Hutchinson's dog, the poor thing. No one knew Mrs. Hutchinson had died until the postman noticed her mail piling up. The police came and when they finally got into the house, they found the dog laying at her feet. Isn't that something? They think she must have been dead for two days or more. The dog was so upset it took the Taylors a while to get her adjusted to their house." Nancy shook her head. "It's awful when you think about it."

Cassie moved her cart further down the aisle. Nancy pushed hers alongside Cassie's.

"And the Batemans, on the other side of your old house, just had triplet boys, if you can believe it. You know they've been trying for years with IVF that never seemed to take. Well, it finally did and look what happened. They sure have their hands full."

Does the woman ever stop talking long enough to breathe?

"And my Derrick just got accepted into Ryerson University, in engineering no less. He'll be leaving home. That bums me out. But Bonnie will be with us for a while. She's a sophomore in high school and in so many clubs I can't keep track of them all. They grow so fast." Nancy finally stopped to take a breath. "By the way, how are your kids?"

The heat returned to Cassie's face. She didn't even know for sure how her girls were faring. "They're good. Both doing great at school." Cassie pretended she saw some clothes she wanted to look at and thrust her cart in that direction. Nancy joined her.

"Just one thing before you go."

Cassie grimaced and decided to face the issue head-on.

"Don't worry. I'll pay back the money I owe you. I haven't forgotten about it."

Nancy waved her hand as if swatting at a fly. "Oh, don't worry about that. That's not what I wanted to ask you."

"Here it comes," Cassie muttered under her breath.

"Where are you folks living now?"

"We found a nicer home down near the lake," Cassie lied. "Nice big back yard for the girls, a home office for Jon and me." Once she got rolling, embroidering on the first lie was easy. "Five bedrooms, four bathrooms. It even has a swimming pool." Cassie did her best to appear nonchalant. "We really don't need all that space, but it's nice to have if we have people visiting us."

Nancy's nose twitched. "How nice." Her voice had taken on the slightest edge. She paused, looked at her phone, and did some scrolling before continuing. "You know, I couldn't help noticing there was a foreclosure notice on your old house. And I saw you with the police one day." She lowered her voice conspiratorially. "Not to be nosy or anything, but what was that all about?"

It took all of Cassie's inner fortitude to maintain eye contact. "Oh, it was just a misunderstanding with the bank. Everything got straightened out. But by then, we'd decided to move anyway. I don't know why they didn't take the notice off the door."

Nancy cocked a groomed eyebrow. "I'd heard some rumors you guys were having financial problems, but I knew it couldn't be true. Both you folks work, and you've never had any problems before."

Cassie's heart thumped so loudly she was sure Nancy could hear it. Her legs grew wobbly and her breaths were more like gasps. Was this what a panic attack felt like? She had to get away from this woman before she passed out.

"Well, that's what it all was—rumors. Everything's fine with us." Cassie took a deep breath to calm herself. "I've got to go now. Someone's waiting for me."

What's one more lie?

The cart's wheels squealed as Cassie pushed it rapidly to the checkout line. She turned around briefly and saw Nancy still standing in the place where she'd left her, her mouth agape.

HOPE DOESN'T DISAPPOINT

Cassie used the self-checkout lane so she could make a speedy retreat. When she reached her car, she yanked open the door, tossed her purchases onto the passenger side, and sank into the driver's seat. Nausea rose into her throat, but she forced it back down. She closed her eyes, squeezing them tightly shut, and then opened them again. For a second, white stars appeared in her line of vision. Then they changed to a word she'd been seeing often in her mind lately, glowing in flashing neon lights like the slot machines.

LIAR.

CHAPTER FOURTEEN

Two months after her arrest, Cassie peeked into the group therapy room at the Halpern Center for Addiction. Four women and six men sat in the chairs arranged in a neat circle. Inspirational posters and information about the services of the Center hung on walls painted a tired beige. A tall man with curly brown hair and dimples leaned on the edge of a desk placed outside the circle. He wore a sports jacket over a golf shirt, blue jeans, and brogues and looked to be the group leader, or facilitator, or whatever the proper term was.

As she walked uncertainly into the room, the man pushed off from the desk and came toward her.

"Are you Cassie?"

He offered his hand, and she shook it. "Yes."

"Good to have you. My name is Ben Gallagher, and I lead the group. Have a seat."

Cassie chose the nearest of the two remaining empty seats. Ben sat down on the other empty chair. Heads bobbed in greeting as her eyes scanned the members. She breathed a sigh of relief to see everyone wore a name tag.

The facilitator offered her a tag and a marker. She scribble-printed her name and stuck the label on the left side of her not-so-clean tee shirt.

"This is Cassie," Ben said. "Each of you please tell her who you are and how long you've been coming here."

The group complied, one by one. When the last person finished, Ben paused a few seconds and then spoke to the participants.

"Because we have a new group member, I thought it might be helpful to start today's session by asking a question some of you have answered before and some haven't. If you've answered it before, it doesn't matter, because you're at a different place now than when you answered the question the last time."

Cassie noticed some of the group members sitting up straighter. Rather than sitting up, Cassie slouched lower and wished a hole would open in the floor so she could disappear.

"If you feel comfortable, I'd like you to close your eyes while I ask you the question, and you think about your answer. Everybody ready?"

Cassie shifted on her seat, wondering what she had gotten herself into. Furtively, she looked around to see if others had closed their eyes. Some had and some hadn't. Cassie decided to keep hers open.

"Suppose tonight you go home after the group, have your dinner, watch television or do whatever you like to do in the evening, and finally get ready for bed. You get into bed and fall asleep. Unknown to you, something wonderful happens while you're sleeping. A problem you've been struggling with, such as addiction to gambling, is gone. But when you wake up in the morning, you don't know that anything has happened. What do you think would be the first thing you would notice as different?"

No one answered for several seconds. Then a thin woman with a long face and frizzy hair spoke up. Her name tag said Joan. "My first thought would be something besides how I was going to pay off all the debt I'm in. I might feel happy instead of depressed."

Ben nodded. "How would you know you were happy?"

Joan thought a minute. "I wouldn't be afraid to answer the telephone because I wouldn't have bill collectors calling me all the time. The call might be from a friend who wanted to know how I was doing."

"So you wouldn't be constantly thinking about the debt you're in, and you'd look forward to telephone calls because they might be from friends and not debt collectors."

"That's right."

"What else do you think you'd become aware of?"

Joan thought a minute. "I wouldn't feel guilty all the time."

"Can you tell us more about that?"

"Well, I know I shouldn't go to the casino. I only lose money. But I always wind up there. Then when I come home, I feel so remorseful, especially if I've lost a lot of money."

"You're saying if the gambling addiction was gone, you wouldn't have to feel guilty anymore. Is that right?"

Joan nodded.

"What do you think you'd do instead of gambling?"

A small smile appeared on Joan's face. "Well, I've always dreamed of writing poetry. I wrote some in high school, and I think a few of my poems were pretty good. But I haven't written much since. If I didn't gamble, I'd have more time to study the art of writing poetry and put into practice what I learn." Joan shrugged. "Who knows? Maybe I'd even become famous."

"That's just it, Joan. You don't know. A dream can take us places we thought we'd never go."

In her mind, Cassie thought about her dreams—dreams of being a good wife, mother, employee. By and large, she'd fulfilled her aspirations. But now, all on her own, she'd smashed those aspirations to bits. They lay like pieces of broken glass, crushed around her feet.

Ben scanned the group. "What about you folks? What would be the first thing you noticed?"

A younger man whose name tag said Frank answered. Blond hair curled around his ears and a few days of dark stubble covered his face. His eyes were the color of milk chocolate.

"I wouldn't be fighting with myself—one part of me obsessing to go to the casino and the other part knowing that going would probably land me further in debt and further away from getting back with my family. And I could look people in the eye because I wouldn't owe them money I had no way of paying back."

Frank paused and stared at the far wall for a long moment. "When I'm gambling, I feel like I'm shut up in a dark prison. I can't get out, and no one can get in. If I didn't have the gambling addiction, I think I'd feel like I'd escaped from jail and come out into the sunshine."

"If I'm hearing you right, Frank, if you didn't have the addiction, you would feel free and be able to enjoy simple things, like the light and warmth of the sun. Correct?" Ben asked.

"Yeah." Frank closed his eyes, then opened them. "In my imagination, I can see myself walking in a meadow full of flowers, and the sun is shining down on my head. It's warm. It feels good."

"It sounds to me like you'd go outside more if you stopped gambling," another group member said. Cynthia was printed on her name tag in large block letters.

Frank looked thoughtful. "Until right now, I didn't realize how much I miss being outdoors."

"I'm kinda like Frank." A heavyset African-Canadian woman spoke. Her name was Carlotta, according to her name tag. She'd drawn flowers around the edges of the tag. Multi-colored ribbons decorated her head full of braids. "Before I started gamblin', I spent a lot of time with my girl cousins. We did all sorts of things together. Now we don't do nothin'." Turning toward Ben, she added, "I'm pretty lonely right now. I've muddled things up so bad with my friends and relatives, they don't come around no more."

"So if the gambling disappeared, you'd feel more positive about getting together with your pals and loved ones. Right?"

"Yeah." Carlotta's eyes filled with tears. "I haven't admitted it before," she murmured, "but 'cause of my gamblin', I've lost friends who were important to me."

Cassie nodded. Like Carlotta, she had lost the most significant people in her life—her husband and daughters.

"Can I ask you a question, Carlotta?" Ben said.

"Yeah, sure."

"What's something you could do the next time you see one of your chums or relations?"

Carlotta thought a minute. "I could ask them to come over to my place. Or meet me at a donut shop."

"Or she could bake some cookies and take them a dozen or two." The suggestion came from a middle-aged woman with a head of long, coarse black hair and eyes as big as silver dollars behind her thick glasses. Her name tag said Irene.

Carlotta grinned. "I like that idea." Then she looked down at her ample body. "Hmm, maybe I should take over fruit and veggies instead."

Giggles erupted around the circle.

"Doesn't matter what you take 'em." The name tag on the speaker's shirt said Jim. He was an older man with a mane of thick, white hair and a bushy beard the color of dirty snow. "Just tell 'em you miss 'em and want to spend time with 'em again. I bet they'll welcome you back."

"I don't know." Carlotta shook her head. "I've hurt some of 'em pretty bad."

"Only one way to find out." Frank had been rocking on the back two legs of his chair. Now he let his chair crash forward with a thump, causing some of the group members to jump.

"I don't know." Carlotta sounded doubtful.

"I've got another question for you," Ben said. "On a scale of one to ten, with one being not likely at all and ten being very likely, how likely are you to take the initiative and make contact with your friends or relatives this next week?"

Carlotta fiddled with her braids. "Maybe a six."

"Why a six and not a five or a seven?"

Carlotta looked thoughtful. "Well, I do want to get back with my buddies and kinfolk. I miss 'em. But I guess I'm afraid. What if they tell me to get lost?"

"What would it take to move you up a notch from a six to say, a six-and-a-half?" Ben asked.

"Hmm." Carlotta started to untie and retie her hair ribbons. "Maybe if somebody came with me, like for support."

The room grew quiet.

"I'll go with you." Cassie blinked in surprise at what came unbidden from her own mouth.

"Really?"

Cassie nodded. "I used to be a buyer for a furniture store, so I'm not afraid of approaching people. We can go together."

"Would you be willing to let us know what happens?" Ben asked.

Carlotta looked uncertain. "What if it doesn't go so good?"

"Not a problem. We'll just look at what you might do differently when you decide you want to try again."

"Okay." Carlotta glanced at Cassie and gave her a nod.

"Is there anyone who sees part of the miracle happening already?" Ben looked around the group.

Jim spoke up. "Well, before, whenever I thought about going to the casino, I'd get all tingly inside."

A few in the group tittered.

He glared at the ones laughing. "Well, I did. Now I don't so much. In fact, some days I don't even feel like going."

"You're saying your desire to gamble has decreased?"

"Yeah, I guess it has. I don't feel as pushed to go to the slots as I did before."

"What's different about not feeling as much urgency to gamble?"

Jim's eyes narrowed. "Well, it gives me time to concentrate on other things."

"Such as?"

"Well, I haven't cleaned my house in probably six months. The other day, instead of going to the casino, I cleaned it from top to bottom."

Carlotta gave Jim a big grin.

"How did you manage that?" Ben asked.

"I guess I told myself if I didn't want to live like a slob, I had to do something about it."

"How did you feel when you were finished?"

"You know something? I felt good about myself. I was so energized, I even cooked myself a decent meal." Jim lowered his head. "Living on my own, I don't eat so good."

"So not going to the casino gave you an opportunity to get things done you'd been putting off, and in addition, to pay more attention to your health."

The corners of Jim's mouth turned up. "It's funny. It didn't dawn on me I was doing something good for myself. But now you mention it, I see I was."

Ben checked his phone. "We're getting near the end of the session. For those of you who didn't have an opportunity to answer the question I posed at the beginning, I want you to write down at least three things you think you'd notice when you discovered you were no longer addicted to gambling. Bring your answers to our session next week.

"And finally, on a scale of one to ten, with one being not at all helpful and ten very helpful, how helpful was our session today?"

"It was an eight for me," Frank responded.

"What made it an eight, Frank?"

"Well." Frank folded and unfolded his hands in his lap. "I'm starting to see how discontented gambling makes me feel. I think I started gambling to make me happy, but it doesn't."

"Any ideas what you could do this week to make you feel happy instead of sad?" Ben asked.

Frank considered. "I could spend some time outside each day."

"On a scale of one not being willing at all and ten being very willing, where would you place yourself on your readiness to do that?"

"Well ... today made me see how much I miss the outdoors, so I think maybe a seven-and-a half."

"Great. If you'd like to share what you did at next week's group session, I know I'd like to hear about it." Ben's eyes skimmed the group. "What about the rest of you?"

"Sure," Jim responded. Other heads bobbed up and down.

Frank nodded his assent.

When each group member had evaluated the session, he dismissed the group. "See you next week, same time and place."

Before leaving, Cassie and Carlotta huddled together to make plans for Carlotta's excursion.

"Who do you want to see first?" Cassie asked her.

Carlotta's face puckered. "I think my cousin Amy. I've stood her up more times than I can count."

"When's the best time to see her?"

"I know she's home Saturday morning because she does her laundry and house cleaning then."

"I'm free Saturday."

Carlotta took a piece of paper and pen from her purse, wrote down the address, and handed it to Cassie. Then she pointed at the piece of paper. "That's an apartment building. I'll meet you at the front entrance at ten o'clock."

"See you then." Cassie turned to go and stopped when Carlotta's hand touched her shoulder.

Carlotta focused her eyes on the floor. "I, uh, appreciate this." She lifted her head and glanced sideways at Cassie. "I don't get a lot of people offerin' to help these days."

"I've burned most of my bridges too." Cassie smiled wryly. "I guess that's why we have to stick together."

"Yeah." Carlotta stared at Cassie a few seconds. "So ... uh ... I guess I'll see you Saturday."

"I'll be there." As Cassie watched Carlotta leave the room, she had to admit it felt good to think about someone other than herself.

"You two get everything worked out?" Ben asked as he approached Cassie.

"I think so."

"I noticed you were pretty quiet today. Any thoughts about your first session?"

"Well … it wasn't as bad as I thought it would be." A tiny smile lifted the corners of Cassie's mouth. "I just may come back."

CHAPTER FIFTEEN

Weary after another twelve-hour day, Deva Ramsaran sat near the window of her restaurant before she closed up for the night. Outside in the dusk, pedestrians hurried home along the sidewalks through the streetlights' warm glow. Just past her seventy-second birthday, Deva rubbed the aching joints in her fingers and elbows and sighed. Today had been a busy day, with crowds of her regular customers and daily first-timers coming in for her Caribbean food with an Asian twist.

She looked around at the interior of her place—Deva's Diner—and at the bright mural of an old-fashioned truck brimming with farm produce bumping down a pot-holed road. At the bottom of the mural an ocean shimmered with sunlight. A woman with chestnut hair—her mother Amelia—rode atop the vegetables. Deva had had the mural specially commissioned.

In Trinidad, young Amelia had helped on her family's farm, walking the long roads to school and then coming home to feed and water the animals, tend the vegetable gardens and pick fruit. In her teens, Amelia saved enough money to purchase the truck. She used it to sell local produce in the neighboring towns.

Amelia and Deva had immigrated to Canada when she was six—Deva never knew her father—and they settled in

Toronto. Its city hustle and noise after the quiet, rural life in Trinidad was unsettling. Often the only child of color at school, Deva's early years in Canada were lonely, getting only moderately better as more immigrants moved into the city. Neither Deva nor her mother ever married, neither finding the right man to share their lives.

After eighty-two years, pneumonia felled Amelia, and Deva nursed her mother through the final months of her life while Deva herself worked as a chef in a midtown restaurant. After Amelia's passing, Deva packed up and left Toronto, resettling in Kettering, on Lake Ontario's shore. She'd opened Deva's Diner three months later. From the start, it had been a success.

She had to stop reminiscing and finish cleaning up and get home to bed. She put her elbows on the table, rested her head in her hands, and closed her eyes.

"Father God, throughout my journey, you've always been faithful. You've never left or abandoned me. In the good times and bad, I've always known you were there. I just wanna say thank you, and tell you I love you, and thank you for Jesus."

Deva opened her eyes and raised them heavenward. "What do you have in store for me next? You always surprise me. Whatever it is, I trust you. I know it'll be good."

CHAPTER SIXTEEN

On a hot summer night, Jon Bailey sighed as he sat in the old recliner in his parents' living room, thankful for the air conditioning. The only thing his mom and dad had changed was the television set he'd grown up with, replacing the old boxy TV with a big flat-screen television mounted over the fireplace. It was a small change compared to the major ones they'd all gone through in the last weeks.

The transition hadn't been easy. His parents lived in the same district where the girls attended school, but they still had to acclimate themselves to their new home environment.

It couldn't be comfortable for his parents, either. His mother and father had established their set routines after all the children had left the nest. They'd been gracious when he asked to move in with them for a spell. He'd assured his father he was searching for a suitable apartment, but his father had said, "No hurry, Son. You can stay here with the girls as long as you need to."

Restless, he went into the kitchen, poured himself a glass of juice, and snagged a cookie from his mom's cookie jar. Everyone else was in bed, and quiet calm had settled over the house. Returning to the recliner, Jon took a sip of his drink and let his mind drift.

As welcoming as his parents were, his father had taken Jon aside for a serious father-to-son talk regarding his situation.

"Make sure you do everything you can to stop Cassie from having any access to your bank accounts or credit cards," his father had said. "Do you still have joint accounts?"

"No."

"What about credit cards?"

"I canceled them. I just use my debit card for now."

"Life insurance?"

"I set up a trust fund for the girls and made it the beneficiary of my life insurance."

Jon's father had seemed satisfied with that.

But constant worries about Cassie, where she was and what she was doing, kept Jon awake at night. She'd called the house a couple of times when he was at work and talked to the girls, but she'd given them no information on where she was living. The phone calls upset them. Jesse summed it up best. "Dad, everything's all scrambled up—like eggs," she'd said.

The girls missed their mother, and he missed his wife. He had to admit it—despite all Cassie had done to jeopardize their family, he still loved her.

How is she surviving?

Cassie wouldn't be eligible for unemployment benefits since she'd been fired for cause. Her car was paid for, so that was an asset she still possessed, if she hadn't gambled it away. Did she spend the night in shelters and eat at soup kitchens? He hated to think what gambling had brought her to, and where she might end up. The look on his parents' faces told him they had similar concerns.

He noticed a small New Testament on the coffee table with some surprise. He'd not had a religious upbringing. He'd read the Bible for one of his university courses because it was required reading, but he hadn't paid much serious attention. He picked up the small volume and turned to the first book, the Book of Matthew. When he reached the verses about God's caring nature, he read them once to himself, and then reread the passage out loud.

> If you decide for God, living a life of God-worship, it follows that you don't fuss about what's on the table at mealtimes or whether the clothes in your closet are in fashion. There is far more to your life than the food you put in your stomach, more to your outer appearance than the clothes you hang on your body. Look at the birds, free and unfettered, not tied down to a job description, careless in the care of God. And you count far more to him than birds.

Jon considered what he'd just read. He liked the part about the birds being carefree because God took care of them. Was God really concerned about him and the muddle he found himself in? Feeling an unnamed need deep inside, he looked toward the ceiling and prayed.

"God, I don't know if you listen to people's prayers, or if you even exist, but I just read where you take care of the birds in the wild. Does that mean you take an interest in me and my family?"

I hope his answer is yes.

He took a deep breath. "Please help us get back on track again." He paused, allowing his thoughts to clear. "And even though nothing's happened yet, I thank you in advance for answering this prayer."

The notion of thanking God for an answer that hadn't come yet suddenly sounded like having faith that God would answer him. He'd always shrugged off the whole idea of faith.

Maybe those churchgoing folks know something I don't.

CHAPTER SEVENTEEN

Cassie stretched her legs out on the backseat of her car. A breeze blew through the open windows, and she took a deep breath of the refreshing air. Parked in the lot of a large mall, she watched people carrying numerous packages struggle to carry them to their cars, often not watching where they were going. This put them in danger of being hit by motorists, jostling with each other for parking spots. Horns honked and shoppers scurried out of the way.

She'd been doing a lot of thinking in the last while. She had to do three things. First, she had to obtain a job. Second, she needed a place to live. Even though it was late summer, a fall crispness hinted at what was to come. And third, she needed to prove to Jon and her children she'd stopped gambling so they could become a family again.

Finding a job proved more difficult than Cassie had anticipated. She knew she wouldn't have much success applying for buyer openings because Lorna wouldn't give her a good recommendation. She decided to apply for restaurant server positions. At the library near her previous home, she prepared her résumé, and she decided to look for a job the old-fashioned way, rather than doing it online. With copies of her résumé in hand, she drove to the downtown district of Kettering, where restaurants and eating establishments lined the streets.

At the first eatery, Cassie only got as far as the hostess at the front door.

"I'm looking for a job as a server." She planted a smile on her face and handed her résumé to the tall, thin woman whose name tag read Linda.

Linda scanned Cassie's résumé quickly and handed it back to her, wrinkling her nose.

"You don't have any experience as a server. We get awfully busy in here, especially during the lunch hour. We need servers who know what they're doing."

"But I learn quickly." Cassie tried rigorously to keep her smile from slipping. She held out the résumé. "Could you at least give it to the manager or owner?" Now she sounded like she was begging.

Linda snatched the résumé. "I will, but it won't do any good."

"Thank you. I appreciate that." She walked sedately out of the restaurant, head held high, trying not to get angry.

The result at the next establishment wasn't much better. This time, Cassie got to speak to the manager, a chunky young Asian man with yellow streaks in his jet-black hair and glasses which kept slipping down his nose. He introduced himself as Eddie. He grasped Cassie's résumé and took a long time reading it.

"It says here you have a degree."

Cassie nodded, hoping that fact would help her land a position.

"You'll never be happy in a job as a server," Eddie said, pushing up his glasses. "As soon as something better comes along, you'll be gone, and I'll have wasted time and money training you."

She shook her head. "I'll stay as long as you want me to."

He stared at Cassie through his thick lenses. "No good. I've seen it time and again. The ones with education? Two months here and"— Eddie snapped his fingers—"poof, they're gone."

"May I call you Eddie?"

The manager nodded.

"Eddie, I really need a job. If you hire me, I won't leave you."

"Can't do it." His voice did not sound unkind. "The owner would have my head."

"Will you at least keep my résumé on file?"

"Sure. But don't get your hopes up."

Cassie gave a half-hearted wave as she walked out the door.

Five other restaurants, ranging from fine dining establishments to holes-in-the-wall gave her the same response—too much education and no experience. She decided to try one more place before quitting for the day, specifically the restaurant with the neon sign flashing Deva's Diner in backlit black curlicue letters.

She went inside. The large windows at the front let in the afternoon sun. A sizeable counter with amply padded bar stools faced the kitchen. A pass-through for the food enabled Cassie to see into the cooking area. Tables and chairs filled the main dining area.

An artist had painted a mural on one wall of an old-fashioned truck carrying farm produce with a woman sitting on top of the vegetables. Miniature wall hangings of blue, yellow, green, and red hung throughout the space, making it cheery and welcoming. A few patrons sat at the tables. Cassie checked her watch and realized it was three o'clock—too late for lunch, too early for the dinner crowd.

She stood still and soaked in the establishment's ambiance until a tiny dark-skinned lady approached her. The elderly woman wore her snow-white hair in a knot on the top of her head.

"Can I help you, my dear?"

"I've come to apply for a serving position." The woman had to be less than five feet tall. Cassie bent down slightly as she held out her résumé to the lady.

"I don't need to see that." She spoke in melodious tones, with only the trace of an accent. She squinted as she looked up at Cassie. "I just want to hear what you have to say for yourself. I'm Deva Ramsaran, the owner." She extended a dainty hand, with rings on all her fingers.

"Cassie Bailey." Cassie shook the woman's hand, worn and calloused in her own. Tongue-tied, she stared at the woman, who scrutinized her from head to toe.

"Well, are you going to tell me about yourself, or are you just going to stand there?"

"Um," she sputtered, "I … uh … have over twelve years of work experience, I learn fast and—"

Tears filled her eyes, and she stopped. Deva waited for her to continue. Finally, the words rushed out.

"And I really, really need a job."

Deva nodded.

A sudden memory flashed through Cassie's mind. "I know I can do hard, physical work because one summer while I was in school, I painted houses for a very demanding boss." When Deva didn't respond, Cassie added, "Not that you'd be demanding or anything."

When Deva reached for her hand and patted it kindly, Cassie couldn't hold back the tears that dripped from her eyes and nose onto her shirt.

Deva handed her a napkin from one of the tables. "I think you've fallen on some hard times. Am I right?"

Blowing her nose loudly, Cassie nodded and hiccupped. "Hard times of my own making."

The owner stared at the mural on the wall. "See that woman sitting on the produce in the truck?"

HOPE DOESN'T DISAPPOINT

Cassie walked over to the mural and looked more closely. "She's very pretty."

"Well, that's my mother, Amelia. She's dead now. I spent the first six years of my life in Trinidad. My mom was a hard worker. True, she made some mistakes in her life, like getting pregnant with me before she was married, but eventually she owned the vegetable truck you see in the picture. And she had the courage to bring me to Canada all by herself."

"I like that story." Cassie wiped her eyes with the damp napkin. "And I like how you have a painting of your mother in your restaurant."

Deva didn't answer but continued to gaze at the mural.

"Well, I won't take up any more of your time." Cassie turned to go.

Deva put a hand on her shoulder. "Where are you going?"

Cassie looked around. "This place seems to run well as it is. I don't think you need any more servers."

"My dear, you're wrong. One of my servers went into labor this morning. I do indeed need another server."

Cassie looked into Deva's eyes and saw an uncommon compassion. "Would you consider hiring me, even though I don't have any server experience?"

"As a matter of fact, I would." Deva smiled. "We'll give it a try for a month. If it works out for both of us, great. You can continue to work here. If not, we'll part ways as friends. Agreed?"

Cassie didn't think it would be possible to be enemies with this woman. "Agreed. When do you want me to start?"

"How about tomorrow morning at eight o'clock?"

"You've got a deal." Cassie offered her hand, and Deva shook it firmly.

As Cassie headed for her car, she gave a little skip.

It's a server job, not the CEO of some big company.

But still, it was a job. She could put a big checkmark beside her first goal. Now she could save for her first and last month's rent and then find a suitable apartment. That would take care of her second goal. Goal three, proving to Jon and the girls she had quit gambling, would be a bit more challenging.

Cassie decided to find a suitable shelter for the night to get herself cleaned up and wash her clothes. Despite the work ahead of her that evening, she hummed to herself as she got into her car. Things were looking up.

CHAPTER EIGHTEEN

Cassie finally found a women's shelter with an empty bed in the west end of town. Maybe it would be better than the first shelter she was in. Located in a nicer area, the building didn't look quite as run down as the previous shelter she'd visited. After completing the intake process, she went to her assigned room and found two metal beds with skinny mattresses butted up against the battleship-gray wall. Dingy worn linoleum covered the floor. She realized her previous assessment of the place had been incorrect. Everything about the place screamed institution.

Cassie tossed her plastic bag of dirty clothes onto the bed and looked over at her roommate, who sat in the room's one chair. The woman, perhaps in her late twenties, nodded but said nothing. Her hair, a mousy brown, hung in greasy strands to her shoulders, and her large hazel eyes held a vacant stare. A sleeve of tattoos covered her left arm. Two silver rings hung from her nose.

"Hello. I'm Cassie." Cassie did her best to sound cheerful.

"I'm Leona." The girl glanced briefly at her and then stared into space again.

Maybe Leona could give her some info about the place. "Have you been here before?"

Seconds passed before Leona shook her head.

"When did you get here?"

"Two days ago."

"Food any good?"

Leona joggled her hand back and forth. "So-so." She rose from her chair and headed to the door. "Gotta go to the john," she said over her shoulder, as she hurried out of the room.

Thankful she had a roommate who wouldn't talk her leg off, Cassie sat on the bed. She glanced over at her overstuffed bag of laundry.

Might as well get the job done sooner rather than later.

Picking up the cumbersome load, she headed for the door. According to her intake process information, the laundry facilities were in the basement.

All the washing machines were in use when she arrived, with three women ahead of her waiting for the next available machine. After several minutes, a buzzer sounded, indicating a machine had finished. Two of the women, one at least six feet tall and the other weighing a good two hundred and fifty pounds, raced for the washer, arriving at the same time.

Beanstalk was faster and started pulling out the clean laundry, dumping it onto the floor and emptying her laundry bag into the machine. Big Girl shoved her out of the way, pulled out the clothes Beanstalk had put in, dumped them onto the floor on top of the first load of clean laundry, and started putting her clothes inside. The third woman waiting seemed as aghast as Cassie at the situation.

Beanstalk body-slammed Big Girl against one of the washing machines. Her face inches from the woman's nose, she hissed like a snake. "I got here first."

Cassie watched in disbelief as the two women punched and clawed each other. Eventually—to Cassie it seemed hours—a shelter worker came running into the room, and with help from Cassie and the third woman, separated the scrappers. The shelter worker held Beanstalk's arms, while Cassie and the other woman pinned Big Girl's arms.

The shelter worker, a tall black woman close to six feet tall and somewhere around two hundred pounds herself, glared at the women.

"Get your clothes and other belongings," she snapped. "You're both outta here. You know the rules. No fighting." After the women gathered up their laundry, the worker frog-marched them out the door as they shouted profanities and blamed each other for causing the altercation.

Cassie and the other lady smiled faintly at each other.

"That added a bit of excitement to the day. Made my hands shake." Cassie held them out for the other to see, then jammed her hands into her pockets to stop the trembling. "By the way, my name's Cassie."

"Helen," the other woman said. "While they were fighting, I heard two buzzers go off, so more washers are open now."

They found the machines that were done and shifted the contents out onto tables, then loaded their own clothes and started the washers. Cassie, not wanting to hang around, decided to explore the shelter while she waited for the machine to finish.

When she returned, she found her clothes strewn over one of the counters, with a few articles on the grimy floor. She gathered up the fallen clothing and shoved all her wet clothes into an empty dryer. Thinking it might be wise to wait for her clothes to dry so she could rescue them as soon as the dryer stopped, she picked up an out-of-date magazine and read a few articles.

Back in her room, as she sorted out the clean laundry, a buzzer announced dinner. Cassie's stomach growled, and she wasted no time heading for the shelter's large dining room. Nearly everyone had been seated when a white woman with bleached blonde hair stood up and started yelling at a woman with brown skin and a pink toque pulled over her ears, who was about to sit in the chair beside her.

"Get away from me. I ain't sittin' beside somebody who's too dumb to know what clothes to wear this time of year."

"Where am I supposed to sit, numb-nuts? All the other places are taken."

"You can sit on the floor for all I care. You ain't sittin' next to me."

Women stood up and formed loose clusters, one group bunched around Blondie and the other around Pinkie. Both sides yelled slurs back and forth. The shouting got louder, and Cassie waited nervously for the first punch to be thrown. When a staff person finally hustled into the room, Cassie expelled her pent-up breath.

"Make her move," Blondie shouted.

"I can't move 'cause there's nowhere else to sit, dimwit," Pinkie shot back.

The staff member propelled the two name-callers out of the room. As the women began to take their seats again, Cassie wondered if the shelter had just gained two more empty beds for the night. When no more arguments broke out, Cassie ate, even though it tasted like sawdust in her mouth.

Later that night, it took her a long time to fall asleep, unused as she was to the sounds and smells of the shelter. Lights-out was at eleven, but that didn't mean the women stopped talking. Chatter filtered into the room and kept Cassie awake. When she finally fell asleep, she tossed and turned on the uncomfortable bed, until she felt a presence near her. She opened her eyes to see Leona standing next to her bed, staring down at her. Cassie sat up quickly, her heart hammering.

"What do you want?"

HOPE DOESN'T DISAPPOINT

Cassie's sudden movement spooked Leona into hopping backwards. When Leona didn't answer her question, Cassie fought hard to control her rising panic. "What do you want?" she asked again, this time more forcefully.

"I don't want nothin'." Leona's voice came out in a monotone. "I was just lookin' at you and thinkin' how pretty you are. I'm not gonna hurt you."

"Well, I'd appreciate it if you stayed on your side of the room."

Slowly, Leona walked back to her bed and sat down on the side.

"I wish I was pretty," she muttered. "My mom always said I looked like something the cat dragged home."

"I'm sorry to hear that." Cassie pulled the covers up to her ears. "But, please don't come near me again."

Ten minutes passed before Leona climbed back into bed. Cassie slept in fits and starts for the rest of the night. When morning finally arrived, after hastily eating breakfast, she gathered her clean clothes and signed herself out of the shelter. As she headed toward her car to start her first day on the job, she didn't know which was worse—living in a shelter or living in her car. She decided both sucked.

CHAPTER NINETEEN

Cassie sat at the two o'clock position in Ben's perfect circle for addicted gamblers at the Halpern Center for Addiction. The place was beginning to feel like home.

She'd worked for two whole weeks at Deva's Diner and received her first pay. What money she needed for living she took out, but the rest she deposited into a newly opened bank account. In addition to two successful weeks of work, she hadn't gambled since she started the job.

Ben smiled as he looked around at the group members. "What's better in your lives since we last met?"

Frank seemed anxious to speak. "Well, I spent time outside every day last week. I didn't miss a day," he said proudly.

Michael, nineteen years old and the youngest member of the group, stood up. His black hair was buzzed on the sides and long on the top, some of it falling into his eyes. His beak nose and wide-set eyes gave him a hawkish appearance. Nonchalantly, he walked over to Frank and gave him a high-five. "Cool, dude!" He nodded at the group before sitting down.

Cries of "Way to go" and "Bravo" echoed from group members.

"Why is your life better because you spent time outside last week?" Ben asked.

"Going outside reminds me there's a whole world out there besides me, the casino, and online gambling." Frank paused and then grinned. "I even said hello to one of my neighbors."

Joan started clapping, and the applause spread around the group. Frank gave a little bow.

"What else is better?"

"Well, I think it's obvious. When I'm outside without any technological gadgets on me, I'm not gambling. And when I'm not gambling, I'm not getting myself deeper into debt."

"What else?"

"I guess you could say when I was enjoying the great outdoors, I felt better about myself. I even got up the courage to call my wife and kids."

"How did that go?" Jim asked.

Frank hung his head. "I've blown things with my wife. She doesn't have much faith in me anymore 'cause I've disappointed her so many times." Cassie could relate to that. Seconds passed before he raised his eyes and looked around the group. "But my kids seemed happy to talk to me."

"You said spending time outdoors shows you there's a whole world out there besides you, the casino, and online gambling. Why is that important?" Ben asked.

Frank looked pensive. "Well …" He stopped for a moment. "Unless you're playing card games, gambling is a very solitary activity. At the slot machines, there are people around you, but you're totally zoned into winning the next jackpot and nothing else. In online gambling, you're playing with people, but you can't see them—you can't make eye contact with them or read their body language. You don't even know their real names." Frank paused before speaking again. "When you think about it, addictive gambling is a very selfish activity—pursuing something relentlessly because you think it will make you happy."

The group was quiet, until Frank abruptly laughed. "You know what? I experienced happiness when I said hello to my neighbor. He looked me in the eye and greeted me. I felt connected."

"Tell me if I'm right, Frank," Ben said. "When you're gambling, you feel alone and disconnected, but when you interact with people, even if it's only a small gesture from someone, it makes you feel connected."

Frank nodded.

Irene adjusted her glasses as she looked around the group. "You know the saying, 'No man is an island' ..." Her voice trailed off and she stared at the tissue she wound in her hands.

"Do you sometimes feel like an island, Irene, alone and cut off from other people?"

"Every now and then."

"What do you do when you feel that way?"

Irene shook her head. "Usually nothin.'"

"What could you do to make you feel less separated from others?"

Nearly a minute passed before Irene responded. When she did answer, she spoke so softly many in the group leaned forward to hear her better.

"Well, I've always liked going to the library. It's quiet and you can take out a book and sit and read. People are around, but you don't have to speak to 'em if you don't want to." She glanced down at the worn tissue.

"You like the peace and quiet of the library and the fact you only have to speak to people if you want to."

"Yep."

"Do you think you'll go to the library this coming week?"

The edges of Irene's mouth formed a miniscule smile. "I might. I have a book that's overdue."

"Let us know next week what you choose to do."

"Okay."

"Thanks for sharing that with us, Irene. I think it took courage on your part, and I admire that."

Two pink spots appeared on Irene's cheeks.

Carlotta twisted one of her braids with her index finger. "Well, Cassie and I went to see my cousin Amy."

"How did that go?" Ben asked.

Carlotta wrinkled her nose. "A little bit good and a little bit bad."

"Which part do you want to start with?"

"The little bit bad." Taking a deep breath, Carlotta continued. "When me 'n Cass got to Amy's apartment, she wouldn't open the door. She told me she didn't want nothin' to do with me."

Michael leaned in. "What did you do?"

Carlotta grinned slyly. "Well, Cass had taken Irene's suggestion and bought some goodies from a bakery. When I told Amy I had treats, she opened the door."

Cassie took up the story.

"It was a little tense at first. Amy took the snacks, and I thought she was about to ask us to leave. But Carlotta got brave and told her cousin she was sorry for all the ways she'd hurt her and asked her cousin to forgive her."

Several group members moved forward on their seats. "Don't leave us in suspense. Tell us what happened next," Jim ordered.

Cassie giggled and then began to belly-chuckle. "Well, I got so involved in what was happening I started to cry. Carlotta commenced bawling, and then her cousin joined in." Cassie stopped laughing and shook her head. "I think we stood there blubbering for at least five minutes. Then

Amy walked over to Carlotta, gave her a great big hug, and told her she forgave her." Cassie paused. "That set the three of us set off sobbing again."

"Wow!"

Heads turned in the direction of the speaker. Her name tag said Brynn. She looked to be in her mid-forties. Extremely thin, she had dirty blonde hair teased into a nineteen-sixties bouffant. This was the first time she had spoken.

"Brynn, what do you think about what Carlotta and Cassie just told us?" Ben asked.

Brynn focused her eyes on the floor and shook her head back and forth. "I don't think I'd ever have the courage to do something like that."

Ben considered her. "It does take a lot of courage to admit we've done something that has hurt someone and to ask for their forgiveness."

The group sat silently for several minutes. Suddenly, Brynn blurted out, "I stole thousands of dollars from my mother so I could gamble." Tears filled her eyes. "I'd like to tell her I'm sorry and that I'm getting some help to stop."

"What would need to happen for you to be able to do that?" Ben queried.

Brynn looked thoughtful. "First of all, I'd have to start talking to her again. I haven't spoken to her for months."

"Would that mean a phone call?" Joan questioned.

Brynn nodded. "That would be a start."

Ben smiled. "Do you think you'll give her a call this week?"

"I'm scared she won't talk to me."

"Is there anything you could do to feel less afraid?"

"She could write out what she wants to say before she calls her mom," Frank suggested.

Ben nodded. "Good idea. Do you think you could do that, Brynn?"

"I can try."

"Is there anyone you'd like to help you?"

Brynn shook her head. "I want to try to write it myself and see how I do."

"Will you tell us next week how it goes?"

Brynn hesitated and then bobbed her head up and down.

Ben checked his phone. "My goodness! We've gone overtime. Is there anything else someone wants to say before you evaluate this session? Speak now, or forever hold your peace. Don't practice the doorknob phenomenon."

His term puzzled Cassie. "What's the doorknob phenomenon?"

"It's the fact clients often leave significant things unsaid until they have their hand on the door handle on their way out."

Cassie smirked. "Well, I'm guilty. I haven't said anything yet, but I got a job and I haven't gambled for the last two weeks." She could feel heat steal up her cheeks.

Cheers burst from the group.

"How did you do that, Cassie?" Ben asked. "How did you get a job, and how have you kept from gambling?"

A thoughtful look appeared on Cassie's face. "When it came to finding a job, I nearly gave up." Cassie lowered her eyes. "Because of some things I've done in the past, I can't get a job in my field. So I decided to look for a server job." She raised her eyes and looked directly at Ben. "Not such a smart move because I didn't have any experience. But I kept trying and finally a dear little old lady hired me. And believe it or not, I like the work."

This time, the group clapped.

"What about not gambling?"

Cassie couldn't help smiling. "I guess I've been so busy learning the ropes of my new job I haven't really thought about gambling."

"How do you think you can keep up your momentum?"

Cassie sighed. "That's the hard part. When I have other things to occupy my mind, I don't think as much about gambling. But I'm not always occupied. That's when the temptation really hits me." She thought a minute. "It also strikes when I'm upset or angry or sad."

"What do you think you can do in those times?"

'Maybe some physical exercise would help, like going for a walk or a jog," Brynn suggested.

Cassie noticed that once Brynn had decided it was safe to speak in the group, she seemed to feel more comfortable participating.

Joan gave Cassie a smile. "Or call a friend."

"I don't have too many of those left."

"What about going to the library and taking out some good books to read?" Frank offered.

Ben turned his attention toward Cassie. "The group has given you some good suggestions, but I want to know what you think would help you."

Seconds passed before she responded. "Somehow, I need to reprogram my brain. It gets excited when I think about winning jackpots, and seeing flashing lights, and hearing tinny music."

"What could you think about instead?"

"I could think about my husband and children. I could think about how much I miss them." Tears welled in her eyes and flowed down her cheeks. Someone offered her a tissue, and she blew her nose.

"I'm going to give you all some information, and I want you as a group to tell me if it's helpful or not," Ben said. "Okay?"

"Tell us." Several members spoke in unison.

"As human beings, when we're faced with something physically dangerous or emotionally upsetting, we have one of two reactions—either a fight response, or a flight response."

Heads around the group nodded.

"Often when things are painful to us, maybe from our past or something that may have just happened, we want to make the pain go away. Our minds come up with something to give us relief. For this group, it's gambling. The desire to lessen the pain arcs—it rises to a crescendo and then it subsides. The length of time that passes from the time the fight-or-flight response begins until it subsides is different for everyone. Learning to ride out that arc until it diminishes can keep us from making the wrong response. Does that make sense to you?"

Cassie thought about it. "I think so."

"What about others?"

"It does to me," Jim responded.

"Me too," Frank added.

Brynn fluffed her hair. "It sounds as if that arc thing is like riding a roller coaster—going up one side to the top and then coming down the other side."

"That's a great analogy, Brynn." Ben turned back to the group. "I'm going to give you all some homework. First, whenever you feel the urge to gamble, I want you to stop and ride it out. Pay attention to how long it lasts. When is it at its worst? How long before the pressure starts to lessen? That's important information to know when the urge hits you off guard. Bring what you discover to the next session.

"Secondly, I want you to cut out pictures from magazines and make a collage of things you believe would be helpful for you to think about or activities you could do while you're riding out that arc of pressure that's building and pushing you toward unhealthy behavior. At the bottom of your collage, write down two or three sentences you could say to yourself while the tension builds. For all who feel comfortable doing it, I'd like you to share your montage with the group and explain why the pictures are meaningful to you."

The group sat quietly.

"Does anyone have any questions?"

When no one spoke up, Ben requested the group members to evaluate the session and then he dismissed them.

Cassie stopped to speak to him on her way out.

"You've given me a lot to think about. You're right about the pressure building. It's like a voice yelling at me to get to the casino so I'll feel better. But it's telling me a lie. I don't feel better—I feel worse. I feel like I'm in a darker place."

"That's why it's important to have tools to combat that voice."

Cassie nodded.

Ben smiled. "I'll be interested to see your collage."

"I will too."

The next day, patrons filled Deva's Diner, and Cassie hurried to deliver their orders. She smiled as she thought about the pay increase Deva had given her.

"I'm real pleased with your work," her new boss had told her, "so I'm goin' to raise your pay by twenty-five cents an hour." Deva's sinewy arms had wrapped around Cassie's waist in a tight hug.

Cassie had bent down and whispered in Deva's ear. "You're the best."

Bella Mae, the head cook, burst into Cassie's thoughts. "Order's up, Cassie."

"Thanks, Bella Mae."

Cassie picked up the order and delivered it to the customer, ensuring she had everything she needed so she didn't have to waste time making an extra trip.

The bell above the front door tinkled, and Cassie turned to see who was entering. A mother and daughter walked in, arm-in-arm. Cassie caught her breath. The girl was about six or seven and wore her hair in pigtails, just like Jesse often did. Mother and daughter looked happy together. Cassie's face grew hot. When the mother bent down and kissed her daughter on her head, Cassie could no longer hold back her tears. Fleeing to the washroom, she pushed open the door, thankful the area was empty. As she leaned against a sink with her back to the door, sobs wracked her body, and she covered her face with her hands.

Suddenly strong arms surrounded her.

"There, there," Deva whispered. "Cry it out, Cassie, cry it out."

"I've made—such a—such a mess of things," she wailed, her breath coming in gasps.

The strong arms didn't move. "Whatever you've done, sweetie, there ain't nothin' that Jesus can't fix."

"I don't think he can fix what I've done."

"He can, dearie, he can." Seconds passed before Deva spoke softly. "Can I pray for you, luv?"

Cassie nodded.

Still enfolding Cassie in her embrace, Deva prayed, "Father God, I don't know what's goin' on here, but you do. The prayer of my heart is that Cassie will come to know your Son, Jesus, who healed the sick, made the blind see, raised the dead, and set the captives free. I pray she'll read your word and see nothin' is impossible with you. I give you praise for all the good things you're going to do in Cassie's life for your glory. I pray this prayer in the precious name of Jesus, Amen."

Cassie didn't know why, but somehow she felt better.

CHAPTER TWENTY

Cassie shivered as the early morning sun shone through her car windshield, making it difficult for her to see. She pulled her coat around her and sat up straighter. The sun was just rising and tones of red, purple, and orange filled the eastern sky. Somehow, the splendor of the sunrise gave her the impetus to face another day. Parked in a strip mall on the outskirts of town, she opened all the car's windows. A crisp fall breeze blew inside—maybe it would blow out the lived-in smells in the car.

After a few minutes, she sniffed the air. The breeze may have blown out the bad smells, but it hadn't blown the stink off her. She sniffed under her armpits and grimaced. She desperately needed a shower. Up until now she'd been taking bird baths in public rest rooms when no one was around and had managed to keep herself clean, but her whole body needed a good scrub with lots of soap and hot water. She couldn't start her afternoon shift smelling like this. But where could she get a shower? She couldn't just waltz into a shelter, take a shower, and waltz out again without a lot of questions and obnoxious paperwork. What to do?

She glanced in her rear-view mirror and noticed a high-rise building two or three streets behind her. A sign on the top said Voyager Hotel. Slowly, a plan formed in her brain.

She'd wait until after normal check-out time at 11:00 a.m. By that point, occupants would have vacated their rooms, often leaving the doors unlocked, but the cleaning staff wouldn't have finished making up all the rooms. She'd enter the hotel as if she was a guest, find a vacated room, and take a nice, hot shower. If she did it fast enough, no one would even notice.

Feeling energized, she headed into the donut shop at the end of the plaza to use the facilities and get herself a cup of coffee. She'd have her shower and then head into work. She'd done her laundry two days previously and most of her clothes were clean. The anticipation of putting fresh clothes on a nice clean body made her realize how long it had been since she'd enjoyed one of the simple pleasures of life.

Just after 11:00 a.m., Cassie put her clothes into a plastic bag along with a hairbrush, comb, and some toiletries, grabbed her purse, and slipped into the hotel. She headed to the elevators and pressed the button for the eighth floor. When she got off, she saw two cleaning carts in the long hallway, one at either end, but no cleaning personnel. She walked slowly along the corridor, checking for unlocked doors. When she found one, she slipped inside. It was evident the room had been vacated. She hurried into the bathroom, hoping the previous occupants hadn't used all the towels. When she found an unused fluffy white towel hanging over the rack, she grinned. Peeling off her clothes, she turned the water to the hottest setting and hopped in.

The water streamed down, prickling her body like pins and needles, and she soaped herself generously. Some shampoo remained in the little bottle offered by the hotel, and she scrubbed her hair until her head tingled. Another bottle contained a small amount of conditioner. She put it on her hair, rinsed it off, and reluctantly turned off the tap. Wrapping herself in the snowy white towel was something she hadn't experienced in a long time. She knew she should hurry, but the softness of the towel was luxurious and she walked out into the room with it folded around her. There were two queen beds and one of them hadn't been slept in. She desperately wanted to climb in and experience what it was like to sleep in a bed again. Instead, she poked her head out the door. The maids' cleaning carts were closer.

Reluctantly, she hurried back to the bathroom, washed her face, brushed her teeth, and blow dried her hair with the dryer the hotel provided. Dressing quickly, she put on a bit of makeup and looked at herself in the mirror. She hadn't looked this good in a long time. She gathered up her belongings and headed to the door. She had just stepped into the hallway when one of the cleaning ladies came out of the room two doors down.

"What are you doing?" She looked surprised and a little startled as she glanced at a chart on top of the cart. "That room has checked out."

Cassie held up her plastic bag. "That's right. I just forgot something."

The woman frowned. "The people in that room asked me for extra blankets yesterday before I left. I didn't see you when I went into the room."

"I was probably in the bathroom."

Not waiting to hear more, Cassie hastened down the hallway. When she turned the corner for the elevators, she ran past them and sped down eight flights of stairs. She didn't stop until she reached her car. Then she doubled over, trying to catch her breath. As soon as she could, she unlocked her car and scooted inside. She scanned the parking lot. No one had followed her. She breathed a sigh of relief.

As suddenly as a geyser erupting, anger washed over her, hot as molten lava. She banged her fist on the steering wheel.

This is all Jon's fault.

If he'd let her come home, she wouldn't have to sneak around in some hotel just to take a shower. As she thought about all that Jon had deprived her of—her children, her home, common comforts—her breathing shortened to angry gasps. Minutes passed before she calmed down. It was then she heard a faint voice in her head, barely loud enough to perceive.

You don't have to live this way. Quit gambling and your life can return to normal.

She dismissed the thought as fast as it came to her mind.

CHAPTER TWENTY-ONE

"Can you explain this to me?"

Jon looked up at his friend and colleague Daniel Marano, parked across the desk from him. They sat in Jon's office, located in a back corner of the dimmed-down closed auto showroom. Jon's New Testament sat in the center of the desk, illuminated only by the security overnight lights. Daniel, a six-foot-five former football tight end with perpetually disheveled hair, was a devout Christian. Jon knew if anyone could answer his questions, this man could.

"Explain what?" Daniel stroked his auburn goatee and regarded Jon with interest.

"The conversation Nicodemus had with Jesus."

Daniel held up a stubby index finger. "Let me run to my office and get my Bible. It's got both the Old and New Testaments in it. We might need to reference both. I'll get one for you too."

When he returned, he placed one of the Bibles in front of Jon and opened the other to the third chapter of the Gospel of John. "Okay, shoot. What's the question?"

Jon leafed to a page and stopped. "I'm going to read part of it, okay?"

"Go ahead."

Jon cleared his throat and began to read aloud.

"'Now there was a man of the Pharisees named Nicodemus, a ruler of the Jews. This man came to Jesus by night and said to him, 'Rabbi, we know that you are a teacher come from God, for no one can do these signs that you do unless God is with him.'"

Jon looked up at Daniel to make sure the big man was listening. He was.

"'Jesus answered him, "Truly, truly I say to you, unless one is born again he cannot see the kingdom of God."'" Jon laid his hands over the page. "What exactly does it mean to be born again?"

Daniel thought a minute before he spoke.

"You're familiar with the story of Adam and Eve, right?"

Jon nodded. "The serpent tempted Eve, and she gave Adam the apple from the tree God specifically told them not to eat from. They got thrown out of the Garden of Eden for it."

Daniel chuckled. "Your summation is correct. God did specifically command them not to eat the fruit of the tree of the knowledge of good and evil, or they would die. Pretty strong command, don't you think?"

Jon nodded again. "I sure wouldn't have disobeyed it."

"But what if a smooth-talking Satan in disguise came to you and said"—here Daniel spoke in a low, theatrical, persuasive tone—"'Hey, Jon, you're getting rooked here. God told you not to eat that fruit because he knows if you do, you'll have his knowledge, and you'll be just like him. And God doesn't stand for any competition.'"

"But God told them if they ate it, they would die, right?"

Daniel spoke in the same smooth-talker persona, waving a dismissing hand.

"Oh no, Jon, you won't die. No, absolutely, you won't die. Trust me. Go ahead, have some of that cool, luscious, juicy fruit. It's all good, Jon. It's all good."

He sat back, his voice its usual tone. "So, you go ahead and eat it. And your eyes are suddenly opened. But you listened to the lies of Satan when he told you God didn't want any competition. He lied when he said it was okay to disobey God." He gave Jon a long, thoughtful look. "By your disobedience—or rather, Adam and Eve's disobedience—all mankind was condemned to die. Not just to physically die, but also to spiritually die."

"But the church says—"

Daniel held up a hand to stop him. "This is where Jesus's statement in John Three comes in—the one saying we must be born again. Jesus is referring to our spirits."

Jon looked puzzled. "But if mankind was condemned to spiritual death because—"

"Give me a minute here." Daniel linked his hands behind his head and leaned back. "After Adam and Eve bowed the knee to Satan and disobeyed God, three things happened. First, their inner spirits died, and every person born into the world after them was born with a leaning toward sin. That includes you and me. Second, instead of the blessings of God covering the earth, the curse of Satan took over and resulted in sickness, poverty, and death. And third, because God is holy, sin separated humanity from God."

Jon scowled. "That's a pretty grim picture."

"It is. But God had a plan." Dan grinned. "God always has a plan. He planned things so we humans could have a relationship with him again."

"How so?"

"Well, through his prophets' voices, God kept saying there was one coming who would fix things for the good. This one would be born of a virgin, someone who would be both all God and all man. This God-man would pay the penalty for sin and provide a way for man to not only have his fellowship with God restored, but to be born again into eternal life. Born again, never to die again."

"God was talking about Jesus then."

"Right." Daniel shifted in his chair. "Satan kidnapped us from God's family with his lies. What happens when a person is kidnapped?"

"Well—" Jon considered. "Usually someone calls and wants a ransom paid for their safe return."

"Right again. Someone has to pay the price—the ransom—to get them back." Daniel sat forward, leaning over the table, his eyes alight. "Jesus ransomed us by his payment of death on the cross. And now, when we put our trust in Jesus and the forgiveness he bought for us with his own life, we're born again. We're adopted back into God's family. Jesus paid the price, and that was God's gift to us here on earth. Our part is to choose to accept God's gift." He held up the stubby forefinger. "And make no mistake. It is a choice. God gave us free will, which means the choice to accept God's gift of redemption through Jesus—or reject it—isn't forced on you. The final decision is yours alone."

He sat back again in his chair, his eyes still bright, smiling at Jon. "And that, my friend, is what it means to be born again."

Conflicting thoughts swirled in Jon's mind. During the arguments among his friends at the university, they said Christians were hypocrites. They said atrocities were committed by Christians in the Crusades and in the burning of witches, the tortures of the Inquisition, and in the sins of slavery. And his friends often asked, "Why would a loving God send people to hell?"

After what Daniel had told him, those university friends were beginning to sound like the smooth-talking Satan, distracting him from God's plan of salvation.

HOPE DOESN'T DISAPPOINT

Jon closed his eyes for a second and then opened them. *I don't really need a Savior, do I?* Sure, he'd done some stupid things in his younger days, like stealing a car and going for a joy ride. And the time he and his buddies sprayed graffiti all over a freshly painted store in the center of town.

Unbidden, unkind things he'd done in the past flashed across his memory. The time he hit a baseball through the neighbor's basement window and blamed his friend. Or the year he'd made the life of a chubby kid in his class so miserable, the child refused to come to school. The times he'd been angry with Cassie—his heart skipped several beats—and the girls. But he'd done good things, too. If his good deeds outweighed his bad deeds, wouldn't that make him right in God's eyes? Wasn't that all that was required of him?

A breeze from nowhere ruffled a couple of pages in the Bible Daniel had laid out for him, and he looked down. The words practically jumped off the page.

"Jesus said to him, "I am the way, the truth, and the life. No one comes to the Father except through me."

No one comes to the Father except through Jesus.

No one.

"Jesus Christ was the final sacrifice for all of the sins of humankind," Daniel said. "That includes your sin and mine, past, present and future." Daniel paused and looked directly at Jon. "Tell me what you think."

Deep down, Jon knew he needed a Savior. He wanted all the nasty things he'd done in his life forgiven, washed away. He wanted to feel clean inside, to make a fresh start.

"I want to make the choice to accept God's gift," Jon said. "I want to be forgiven. I can't live any other way."

Daniel nodded solemnly. When he spoke, his voice was low. "I'm going to pray a prayer, and I'll say it slowly, so you can repeat it after me, okay?"

Jon nodded, and they bowed their heads.

"Mighty God, I come to you a sinner. Thank you, dear Father, for sending your Son to earth to save me. I believe in my heart and confess it now that you, dear Father, gave your only Son as payment for my sins, and then raised him from the dead. I accept your gift of forgiveness, and I ask Jesus into my heart so I may be born again. Father, I pray this prayer in the name of Jesus. Amen."

The two men looked at each other after the amen, tears running down their faces, and embraced in a bear hug.

"You don't know how long I've been praying you'd do this." Dan's voice sounded husky. "Today the angels in heaven are rejoicing over you."

"Thank God," was all Jon could manage.

CHAPTER TWENTY-TWO

Sleeping in the car stressed Cassie out. Did people look in her windows while she slept? Would they break in and harm her? Tonight, her car sat in a commercial part of town. In the back seat, she rolled from her side onto her back, and pulled a tattered old blanket she'd brought from home up to her chin. Light from the nearby street lamp made the condensation on her windshield glisten. Fog had blown inland off the lake, and in the darkness the buildings rose from the ground like giant box monsters. Restless, and still trying to get comfortable, she flipped onto her other side and closed her eyes.

An elevator stood before her. She entered it. Without her pressing any buttons, it started rising. Where was she going? She had to get off. She pressed the buttons, but nothing happened. Then suddenly, the elevator crashed to the ground.

Cassie sat up in a panic and looked out her rear window just in time to see two men loading tires and rims into a van before driving away. She strained to see their license plate number but the vehicle was too far away. Minutes passed while she waited for her heart to calm down. Then she got out and circled her car. On both sides at the back, her brake rotors rested on the pavement. Her tires and rims were gone.

"What am I going to do now?" she wailed. Only silence greeted her.

Climbing into the back seat again, she lay down. A million considerations raced through her mind. She didn't have enough money for new tires and rims, or even to pay for a tow. Her car had to be functional. It was her home. The thoughts orbited round and round, exhausting her. In the morning, she woke up to a gray sky, drizzle, and a hammering headache. She sat up and saw cars pulling into the parking lots of the commercial buildings. Checking her watch, she saw it was after 9 a.m. She had slept in.

She hurried to a restaurant not far from where she parked. She needed to use the washroom and hoped the place was open. The woman at the front counter nodded to her when she entered, and Cassie pointed toward the rest rooms. She freshened up, put on a bit of makeup, and then went out and sat at a booth, trying to figure out what her next move should be.

The server arrived and she ordered a cup of coffee and a muffin. Although she had insurance, she didn't want to make a police report. She'd had enough to do with the police. Sipping her coffee, she remembered she had automobile assistance. Was it still valid? She pulled her wallet from her purse, yanked out the card, and examined it. Valid for another month. Something was working in her favor.

She finished her coffee and muffin and paid her bill. When she asked if she could use the telephone for a local call, the woman brought the phone over to the counter. Cassie called her auto assistance company and told them her story.

"You're going to need a flatbed truck, lady."

"Is that more expensive?"

"Yep. But depending on your coverage, you may not have to worry about it. What kind of car you got?"

"A Honda Accord."

"They always go for the Hondas."

Great.

"How long until you get here?"

"Forty-five minutes to an hour. It's been crazy this morning. Lots of car accidents with the drizzle."

She gave him the name and address of the restaurant and told him she'd come outside as soon as she saw the truck.

An hour and a half passed before the truck pulled up in front of the restaurant. Cassie hurried out and climbed up into the front seat beside the driver, who introduced himself as Gary.

"My car's just down there." She pointed.

Fortunately, no one had parked in front or behind and the driver pulled his truck in front of her car. She held her breath as she watched him maneuver the Honda onto the flatbed, praying that nothing got damaged. After it was done, the driver looked at her. "Where to?"

Cassie hadn't thought about that. "Do you know a nearby place that sells wheels and rims for a decent price?"

The driver, a heavy man with a balding head and ruddy complexion, picked up his cell phone and scrolled. "There's a tire shop not far from here. Want me to take you there?"

"Sure."

When they arrived at the store, Gary glanced over at Cassie. "I'll wait while you go in and talk to them. See if they got what you need."

The shop consisted of a long counter with three men behind it. To the rear of the men, she saw three bays with hoists. People milled around, waiting for their cars. One of the service guys beckoned her over and she walked up to him.

"How can I help you?"

"The rear tires and rims on my car were stolen. I need new ones."

"What size?"

Cassie frowned. "I don't know."

"What's the make, model, and year of your car?"

When Cassie told him, he checked his computer. "You need 17-inch rims. What kind of tire do you want?"

Cassie shrugged. "What's the cheapest you've got?"

The man pressed more keys on the computer. "You can get an all-season radial for two hundred bucks."

Four hundred dollars she didn't have, plus installation and tax.

Sweat formed under Cassie's armpits. Somehow she had to come up with the money. On the way over to the tire place, she'd noticed a pay day loan company.

"I've just got to go to the bank and I'll be right back. Can you hold a pair for me?"

"Sure, lady."

"When can I get the work done?"

The man glanced at his computer. "It's noon now. I can fit you in at 2 o'clock."

Cassie breathed a sigh of relief. That would give her time to get to the pay day store, arrange a loan, and get back again.

She hurried out to the tow truck and spoke to Gary. "They can do it for me."

"Good. I'll get the car off."

Again, Cassie watched with trepidation as Gary offloaded her car. When the job was safely completed, she asked if he could drop her off at the pay day shop down the street.

"Sure. Hop in."

It didn't take long to get to their destination. Cassie thanked Gary profusely and jumped out of the truck. He waved before pulling out into traffic.

HOPE DOESN'T DISAPPOINT

A long line awaited Cassie inside the store. No one looked very happy. She didn't feel very thrilled herself. When she reached the front of the line, the customer service representative eyed her up and down. Her cheeks burned with heat. "How much?" he barked at her.

Cassie had forty dollars cash with her and one hundred dollars in her bank account, which she needed to live on. She didn't want to borrow a cent more than she had to. "Four hundred dollars."

The man proceeded to ask her a list of questions, keying her answers into the computer. Within minutes, her loan was approved. As she walked out of the store with four crisp hundred-dollar bills stuffed in her purse, she glanced at the paperwork she'd grabbed on her way out. A line at the bottom caught her eye. The annual percentage rate of the loan was 391.07%! Her eyes bulged. Was that even legal? She'd have to pay off the loan the minute she got her next pay.

The trek back to the tire store took her almost an hour, striding into the wind. As she walked into the store, she checked her watch. One-fifty-five. She'd made it on time. She walked over to the same gentleman who had served her earlier. After completing the paperwork, he told her the total cost came to four-hundred-and-thirty-five dollars. She handed the man the bills and sat down on a cracked vinyl chair to wait for her car. She'd almost nodded off to sleep when someone spoke to her.

"She's all set."

Cassie looked up to see a tall man wearing coveralls. He had dark brown hair and a bushy auburn beard. He handed Cassie her keys. "Your car's out back."

"Thank you."

"No problem. Heard you had your rims and tires stolen. Better be careful where you park."

Cassie walked around to the back of the shop and got into her car, dog-tired after an anxious day of running around to get her car operational again. The tire technician's words echoed in her mind. When she thought about it, nowhere was safe to park. Living out of her car wasn't safe. She had to get into an apartment. And with this setback, it would take longer than ever.

CHAPTER TWENTY-THREE

Cassie's feet were falling off. Every table at Deva's Diner was filled, and it was only eleven forty-five. It seemed as if everyone yearned to be out in the fresh October air. When they were hungry and weary from their travels, they wanted to come to a restaurant that served comfort food. Deva's restaurant fit the bill perfectly. The delicious aroma of Caribbean and Asian food filled the place, making Cassie hungry. She and the other servers hustled from table to table, keeping service running smoothly.

Cassie approached a table with three men in business suits and took their orders, repeated the orders back, and delivered beverages and bread. She brought their orders twenty minutes later, and in the process accidentally knocked over a glass of soda belonging to the oldest of the three men. The sugary liquid spilled onto his trousers and ran down his leg, cutting the diners' conversation short and enraging the older man, who jumped to his feet.

"You stupid woman, what's the matter with you? This is a brand-new suit!"

Grabbing some napkins, Cassie tried to soak up the spill from the table. "I'm so sorry." Without thinking, she attempted to wipe the stain on his pant leg. He pushed her away, making her stumble.

"Get away from me!"

By now, everyone in the restaurant gawked at the cause of the commotion. Cassie's cheeks burned.

Deva hurried over. "I'm sorry for what happened, sir. We'll be happy to pay for your dry-cleaning. And your meals are on the house." She stopped and craned her neck to look up at the man, who was a good foot taller than her. "Sometimes accidents happen." She turned to Cassie and gave her a reassuring smile.

"This suit is cashmere, if you know what that is," he snarled. "It cost me a fortune, and it's ruined. Forget the meal—I'm leaving. I'm sending you the bill for a new suit." He wagged his finger at Deva, his face beet red. "In future, make sure you don't hire dumb twits for servers."

The other two men tried to persuade their colleague to stay, but he stomped toward the exit. Reluctantly, nodding their silent apologies, his cohorts followed him out the door.

Deva turned to her customers. "I'm truly sorry for all the hubbub. Everyone gets a free sundae for dessert."

Cheers erupted around the room as people returned to their food. Deva put her arms around Cassie.

"You didn't do anything wrong, sweetie. It was an accident."

Cassie couldn't stop her tears.

"Aw, luv, do you want to leave?"

Taking a napkin, Cassie wiped her eyes. "No. I'll stay."

"Sure?"

Cassie nodded, still trembling inside. The man's words rang in her ears as her father's had, telling her she never did anything right and she'd turn out just like her mother. His carping about the apple not falling far from the tree still echoed in her mind.

As soon as the shift ended, Cassie made a beeline for her car. She didn't want anyone or anything to get in her way. Squealing her tires, she headed to the casino, completely forgetting what the group for addicted gamblers had discussed about waiting for the pressure to gamble to subside.

When she got to the casino, she found only twenty dollars in her purse. Loading the money into the machine, she played until it was gone. She nearly tapped her bank account when shame inundated her.

She buried her face in her hands. She'd done so well for the past weeks, and now she'd blown it. The goal of proving to her family she'd stopped gambling kept moving farther away.

Picking up her purse, she headed to the exit and got into her car. She longed to hear her daughters' voices. The library's entryway had a pay phone, so she headed in that direction and parked nearby. She maxed the parking meter time, not wanting to get more parking tickets. She never wanted to see another parking ticket as long as she lived, or serve jail time for not paying one.

Cassie frowned at the grubby telephone. Pay phones were a pain. She decided she would purchase a cheap, refurbished cell phone with a pay-as-you-go plan. She fed coins into the fractured plastic unit, their falling clinks reminding her of an old-fashioned slot machine. After four or five rings, Anne-Marie picked up.

"Hello." She spoke so softly Cassie had to strain to hear.

"Hello, sweetheart. It's Mom. How are you?"

"I'm okay."

"How was school today?"

"Good."

"Tell me about it."

"We had fun playing hide and seek at recess. No one could find me until I came out of my hiding place. After that we jumped rope."

"What else was good?"

"Every day after lunch, the teacher reads a book to us. When she stops reading and we have to do something else, I want her to keep going so I can find out what happens next."

Cassie smiled. "I'm glad you're enjoying it. Anything else you did today that was fun?"

"No."

After an awkward silence, Cassie asked, "Is Jesse there? I'd like to say hi to her too."

"No. She had a toothache, and Grandma took her to the dentist. Grandpa's upstairs working in his office."

Cassie closed her eyes and rubbed her throbbing temples. Her daughters were hurting, and she was not there to help them. Neither mother nor daughter spoke for several seconds, until Anne-Marie's breath sounds turned to sobs.

"Mom, when are you coming home?" she wailed. "I don't want to live with Grandma and Grandpa anymore. I want us to be a family again."

Choking sounds escaped from Cassie's throat. Hearing her daughter's sobs and not being there to comfort her broke Cassie's heart.

"What's the matter with you, anyway?" Anne-Marie's tone had moved from sorrow to anger.

Seconds passed before she answered.

"I have a problem, sweetheart, and Daddy doesn't want me to come home until I'm better."

"Then it's his fault everything's all messed up."

"No, it's not Daddy's fault. The fault is all mine."

Sobs and hiccups traveled over the phone. Cassie ached to provide her daughter with some hope.

"I am doing something to try to get better."

"How long's it going to take?"

"Hard to say, honey. I wish I could tell you, but I can't."

Just then, Cassie heard footsteps and commotion on the other end of the line.

"Grandma and Jesse are home," Anne-Marie announced. "I gotta go." Before Cassie had a chance to ask how Jesse's tooth was, Anne-Marie banged down the phone.

Cassie's heart landed in her stomach.

"I have to quit gambling." Tears spilled out of her eyes and ran down her cheeks. "My daughters need me. I've got to quit."

CHAPTER TWENTY-FOUR

Cassie took a deep breath before sharing her montage with the addicted gamblers group. She hoped the participants understood it. Ben had requested each group member tape their work to the wall and comment on it, when it was the member's turn to reveal what they had done. Her hands trembled, and she had difficulty getting the tape to stick to the wall in the last open spot. When she finally managed it, she looked at her work and then out at the group who watched her expectantly.

Pictures of families participating in various activities—swimming, hiking, skating, eating a meal together, visiting a museum, tobogganing, watching animals in a zoo—covered every square inch of the board. At the bottom of the page, she had written two words—Anne-Marie and Jesse.

A sketch of a woman standing outside a house looking through a window at a family eating dinner had been pasted in the center.

"Tell us about this," Ben requested, pointing to the woman.

"Well ..." Cassie stopped as tears welled in her eyes. "Because of gambling, I'm not with my family right now. I need to convince my husband I've stopped gambling before he'll allow me to return home. So, when the pressure to gamble is almost intolerable, I should think about my family and how important they are to me. Because unless I stop gambling, I'll always be on the outside looking in."

"What's that like for you, Cassie?"

"Awful." The word came out as a wail, and tears streamed down her cheeks. "I feel like half a person. I belong with my family. They're part of me."

Carlotta handed Cassie a handful of tissues.

"Do you think about your family when you gamble?" Ben asked.

Cassie hung her head. "Not so much."

"Why do you think that is?"

Raising her head, Cassie stared at him. "I guess I thought I could still gamble and be with my family at the same time. But my husband is adamant. He won't take me back until he knows for sure I've quit."

"I see sadness in your eyes. Is there something else you want to share?"

"The other night, I went back to the casino and gambled at the slot machines."

"Can you tell us about it?"

Cassie took a deep breath. "Well, I think I've already told the group about my new job. I work in a restaurant as a server." She paused. "The owner's been good to me."

"What happened? Did you get fired?" Jim asked.

She half-smiled through her tears and shook her head. "No, not fired. I accidentally spilled a glass of soda on a customer's expensive suit. He yelled at me, made a big scene in front of the other patrons, and stomped out of the restaurant." She rubbed her temples. "It really upset me."

"What did you do?"

"As soon as the shift ended, I headed for the casino." Cassie focused on the floor.

"And?" Irene peered at Cassie over the top of her eyeglasses. "Don't leave us hanging."

"I fed twenty dollars into a slot machine and won nothing."

"Only twenty bucks?" Mike asked.

Cassie nodded. "It was all I had with me."

"Did you take money out of your bank account, or try to borrow money so you could keep gambling?" Ben asked.

"No."

"What kept you from doing either of those things?"

A far-away look appeared in Cassie's eyes. "Well ... I just felt ashamed of myself. After I left the casino, I spoke to my oldest daughter on the phone, and she asked me when I was coming home. She seemed so unhappy." Cassie stopped and cleared her throat. "It really broke me up."

The room was silent.

"If I don't stop gambling," Cassie said, "I won't have a relationship with my kids. I won't be with the people I love." She bowed her head and wept. Carlotta, sitting next to her, reached over and hugged Cassie, stroking her head.

Ben gave her a few minutes before he spoke. "So, it sounds to me thinking about the consequences of gambling, especially regarding your children and family, is a motivator to stop gambling. Am I right?

Cassie nodded.

"What else, Cassie?"

"Gambling is a deceiver, a liar." She stopped and cleared her throat. "When I'm upset, I think it will make me feel better. It does for a while, but in the end it makes my life a whole lot worse. Somehow I have to get that into my thick skull."

"Anything else?" Ben spoke softly.

"I have to figure out what's more important to me, gambling or my family, because I can't have both."

"Anything else?"

With tears stinging her eyes, Cassie scanned the group members. "I was afraid to tell you I'd gambled again. I thought everyone would look down on me."

"Oh, honey," Joan said, her voice compassionate. "How could we look down on you? We've all been there. We've all slipped back, but we're on this journey together. That means we support each other. We've shared our telephone numbers with each other. If you feel the urge again, just call me."

"Or me," Irene added.

"Or me," Carlotta offered.

"You can even call me if you want," Jim said somberly.

The group chuckled.

"Well, she can." Jim folded his arms. "I mean it."

Ben waited until the group settled down. "Cassie, anything else you want to say before we wrap up?"

"You guys are like another family to me, a caring, supportive family." After a moment she added, "And that feels good. Thank you all."

CHAPTER TWENTY-FIVE

A week later, Cassie stood in the library entrance again to make another pay phone call. Every time a patron entered the building, the stiff, cold breeze made her shiver. The entryway's gray concrete walls were stark and chill and depressing. Dank, moldy odors seeped from the cracked flooring. After dialing, she paced back and forth the length of the telephone cord, waiting for Jon to answer.

"Hello."

"Jon, it's Cassie. Can we meet somewhere?"

Cassie could hear Jon breathing. Thinking of an excuse.

"Uh ... it's hard for me to get away from work right now. Can we do this later, maybe tonight after the girls are in bed?"

The lines around Cassie's mouth tightened into a frown. "I'd really like to do it now."

Jon sighed. "Okay. Meet me in thirty minutes. The diner around the corner from the dealership."

"Sure." Cassie hung up with a bang. A library user entering the building gave her a quizzical stare. As he passed, Cassie made a face behind his back.

She found Jon sitting in a rear booth at the diner. Her shoes clacked on the wooden floorboards as she walked briskly to the booth and slid in across from him.

"This place hasn't changed much," she said as she looked around. The same pictures hung on the walls, and the same aroma hung in the air—brisket slow cooking in the roaster, ground beef and pork patties sizzling on the grill, onion rings hissing in the deep fryer.

"Would you like something to eat?"

Cassie shook her head. "Just a diet cola."

"I think I'll have some coffee and a piece of their strawberry rhubarb pie."

After the server took their orders, Jon scrutinized Cassie. "You look like you've lost weight."

Cassie looked down at herself. "Maybe a bit."

"Are you eating all right?"

"Yes. I have a job as a server in a diner. The owner lets me eat my meals there."

Jon tilted his head in a question. "You're working as a server?"

"Yeah."

Seconds passed before Jon spoke. "What was it you needed to see me about?"

"I want to come home." She told him about the previous week's phone call, about Anne-Marie's crying and Jesse's toothache.

"Anne-Marie asked me when I'm coming home, Jon, and I didn't know what to tell her." Tears blurred Cassie's vision.

Their order arrived. Jon took his time stirring cream and sugar into his coffee. He took a measured sip and set his cup on the exact center of the napkin with exaggerated slowness.

"Just like nothing has changed in this diner," he said, "nothing has changed between you and me. When I'm convinced you've stopped gambling completely, then we can talk about becoming a family again."

Cassie banged her fist on the table and glared at him. "I'm getting help, Jon. I go to a group for addicted gamblers every week. I've got a job. What more do you want?"

Jon took a bite of his pie and offered some to Cassie. She shook her head. "Too bad. It's scrumptious," he said, taking another mouthful.

Cassie glared at her husband's casualness. "Are you even listening to what I said? What do you want from me?"

He took his time chewing and swallowing the bite of pie before he spoke. "When's the last time you gambled?"

Cassie's eyes veered toward the wall.

"Not that long ago, was it?"

"Um ... well ..." Cassie didn't finish her sentence. The silence between them settled like a thick fog.

Minutes passed before Jon unexpectedly snapped his fingers. "I have to tell you. Something wonderful has happened to me, and I want to share it with you."

She bristled at the abrupt change in the conversation.

"I'm not sure where to start." He stared at Cassie, a thoughtful look in his eyes. "I was sitting up late one night after my parents and the girls had gone to bed, and I found a New Testament lying on the coffee table."

Cassie shrugged at him and held both hands up as if to say so what?

"I have no idea how it got there, but I started reading it." Jon paused. "Maybe because of all the turmoil we've been going through."

The heat in Cassie's chest rose and bloomed on her cheeks.

"I came to the Gospel of John, where Jesus tells Nicodemus, a religious bigwig of his day, he must be born again."

Great. Now he's a holy roller.

"You haven't gone and gotten all religious on me, have you, Jon?"

He ignored her question. "You remember Dan Marano from the dealership, right?"

"Of course."

"Well, he's a committed Christian, and I asked him some questions about what I'd read. The long and short of it is that I've asked Jesus to be the boss in my life."

Cassie rolled her eyes. "I knew it. Mister Holier-than-thou Jonathan Bailey."

Jon smiled. "No. Not that. I'm definitely not a goody two shoes. But when I prayed and told Jesus I accepted his forgiveness and invited him into my life, something inside me changed. I felt free, like I was starting all over again." Jon looked into Cassie's eyes. "Wouldn't you like to begin all over again?"

Anger exploded inside her, white-hot.

"The only thing I'd like to start over again is to come home and be a mother to our children. Right now they need me, Jon, and I need them. Not religion. Them."

Jon shook his head. "They need a mother who doesn't gamble. And until I know you've quit, our living arrangements stay the same."

Cassie banged her empty glass on the table. "How could you keep your daughters away from their mother? What kind of a pompous know-it-all are you? What kind of a father?" She snorted in disgust. "And you call yourself a Christian?"

Several patrons looked around to see the show. Ignoring the onlookers and his wife, Jon took another slow drink of coffee before he answered.

"I understand you're upset. But as I said before, for now things stay as they are."

Cassie jerked to her feet. Her words crackled in the air.

"You think you're so much better than I am, keeping my daughters and me apart. I won't let you get away with it." She brought her face to within inches of his, her voice a blade slicing the air between them.

"You are one despicable man, Jon Bailey."

Turning, she headed toward the front door, slamming it on her way out, and headed for her car.

Once inside the casino, she concentrated on nothing but winning.

CHAPTER TWENTY-SIX

At three-thirty the next morning, Cassie left the casino and headed to her father's apartment. She couldn't remember how long it had been since she'd last visited him. When she arrived, she nearly tripped over a beer bottle hidden in the grass as she walked toward the building entrance.

Dread made her legs wobbly. She couldn't get enough air. Inside, her tracing finger raced down the names in the entryway. The label for Harry Anderson was still in the same place. When she reached her dad's apartment, lines of perspiration streaked her forehead. She leaned against the wall to give her heart time to slow down, then doubled over as remorse and panic took hold. Tears dripped from her cheeks onto her clothes and from there to the floor.

Minutes passed before she regained composure enough to stand up straight and knock. When her father didn't answer, she banged louder. A lady in a tattered housecoat two doors down stuck her head out and made a lewd gesture at Cassie.

"Stop the racket. We're trying to sleep in here." Then she went back inside, slamming the door shut. Cassie ignored the woman and knocked again. On her third try, her father opened the door, wearing boxers and an undershirt, his hair sticking out at odd angles, his eyes bloodshot.

"Cassie, what are you doing here? It's four in the morning."

"The place I've come from doesn't have clocks." She began to sway. Her father reached out and supported her as he led her to his threadbare couch. He forced her to lie down, picked up a grimy pillow from the recliner nearby, and put it under her head.

"Let me put on a pair of pants. I'll be back in a minute."

When he returned, he'd put on pants and a plaid shirt. He brought over a chair and sat. "What's the matter, Cass? You look like you've seen a ghost."

She tried to sit up, but her father gently pushed her back down. "Are you sick? Have you been in an accident?"

She propped up on unsteady elbows. "I've just done something foolish, Dad, and I need to borrow some money."

"What do you mean, done something foolish?"

Cassie shook her head and lay back down.

"I want to move into an apartment, and I finally saved up for my first and last month's rent, but I've lost the money. If I don't put the money down soon, the apartment I'm interested in will be gone."

"What do you mean, you've lost the money? And why are you getting an apartment? You and what's-his-name having trouble?"

"Never mind, Dad. It doesn't matter. Can you loan me two thousand dollars?"

Her father moved forward on his chair. "That's a fair chunk of change."

Cassie nodded. "Can you loan me the money?"

"I don't have it."

She sat up. "What do you mean, you don't have it?"

"A friend recently persuaded me to invest in some stocks he said were going to skyrocket." Harry swore. "All the stocks he recommended have landed in the basement. I've pretty much lost the little nest egg I'd saved up."

Desperation rose in Cassie's chest.

"Couldn't you take out a loan? I'll pay you back."

Harry looked closely at his daughter.

"You know, girl, it seems strange. You don't see me for months. And now you come knocking on my door at four in the morning, looking like you've been in a train wreck, asking to borrow money to rent an apartment. What's going on?"

Cassie punched the couch with a white-knuckled fist. "Dad, this is important. Please help me, please." Even as she said it, she hated the begging tone in her voice.

Her father shook his head. "I told you. I don't have it. And even if I did, I'm not sure I'd hand it over to you. Looks to me like you've found yourself in money trouble, and you won't tell me why."

"Does it matter what I did?"

"Cassie, you seem really upset. I think you ought to stay here tonight. I have some clean sheets. I'll bring them out to you." He stood up. "We'll hash this out in the morning."

"No way. If you can't loan me money when I need it, why would I accept your—how should I say it—hospitality?" She bit off the last word and used her fingers to put air quotes around the word hospitality. She moved toward the door, staggering from fatigue and stress.

"Thanks for always being there for me, Dad." Her voice dripped sarcasm. She opened the door and stepped into the hallway. "You were never there for me. Never."

Halfway down the hall, she turned and saw her father staring after her, a look of bewilderment on his face.

"Thanks, Dad. Thanks a lot."

The words echoed up and down the corridor as Cassie stumbled away.

CHAPTER TWENTY-SEVEN

Somehow, Cassie had to recoup the money she'd saved for her apartment's first and last month's rent. Here at the end of October the nights were getting chilly. Snow would be falling before she knew it. She couldn't live out of her car in the cold weather.

After spending two days considering her options, she entered the Orlando Pawn Shop in downtown Kettering. Once inside, the first thing she noticed was the odor of old socks and unwashed sports equipment. The shop appeared to be empty of employees, and she moved along the shelves, peering down at jewelry, old coins and paper money, knives, dishes—she could barely take it all in.

Five minutes passed before a corpulent man entered from the back. He had a head full of snow-white hair and a bushy gray moustache. His constantly moving deep-set dark eyes and hooked nose reminded Cassie of a vulture.

"Can I help you?"

Seconds passed before she slowly tugged off her engagement ring.

"I'd like to pawn this." Her voice cracked as she met the man's eyes.

"Hmm. Let's see what you've got there."

He took a jeweler's loupe from a drawer and scrutinized the diamond, turning it back and forth in his hand.

The diamond was three-quarters of a carat, round cut, and set in fourteen carat gold. When Jon had placed the ring on the third finger of her left hand so many years ago, she'd always felt such pleasure whenever she moved her finger and the diamond sparkled. And now she was pawning the symbol of their love and commitment.

A burning sensation traveled from her chest to her forehead. How had her life come to this? She nearly reached out and snatched her ring from the man's chubby hand. Taking a deep breath, she told herself she would buy it back as soon as possible.

"I can give you seven hundred for it."

"My husband paid fifteen hundred, and that was over twelve years ago. It's got to be worth more than that now."

The man shrugged. "How many people want a used engagement ring?"

"It's worth at least a thousand."

"The most I'll give you is seven hundred fifty. Take it or leave it."

The amount was nowhere near what she needed for her first and last month's rent.

Cassie nodded her assent. The man checked her identification and went to the back of the store. He clicked some keys on a computer, printed off a form and brought it back for Cassie to sign. As soon as she'd written her signature, he counted seven hundred fifty dollars into Cassie's hand. She stuffed the money into her purse.

"Remember, if you don't buy it back in thirty days, it goes up for sale. And interest will be added to the price."

"Those are the terms?"

"Lady, read the paper you just signed. It's all spelled out." He pointed to the document scrunched in her hand.

"Okay."

He offered his hand and Cassie reluctantly shook it.

"Nice doing business with you." He gave her a satisfied-vulture smile.

Her soul black with despair, Cassie turned on her heel and left.

CHAPTER TWENTY-EIGHT

A week after Cassie's encounter with her father and the pawnbroker, she sat in the passenger seat of her car near midnight, at the corner where Carleton Street crossed Main. She opened the car window, stuck her head out, and stared up at thousands of stars glimmering in the night sky.

So beautiful.

So cold, and so distant.

Her life was in shambles. She'd saved enough money to rent an apartment and then gambled it away. She'd pawned off her diamond ring, but the money wasn't enough. Getting back with Jon and the girls was impossible.

Worthless.

Worthless.

Worthless.

If she couldn't be with her family, she had no reason to go on with such a futile existence. Her husband and daughters obviously didn't need her. They'd done okay so far. They hadn't come looking for her. She leaned her head back against the headrest, weary of listening to the condemnation inside her head.

Thirty minutes later, a siren jolted her awake. Her mind struggled to sort through its half-awake jumble until one clear thought emerged.

No one cares where I am tonight. No one worried about her. She meant nothing to them. She was no use to them except maybe as a brick tied around their necks.

Worthless.

Cassie pulled some tissues from the box beside her and flattened them on her lap. One by one, she counted out twenty-five 500-milligram acetaminophen tablets onto the tissue. She opened the bottle of apple juice she'd bought. She alternated swigs of juice with pills from the small pile until both were gone. She leaned back and closed her eyes.

Scenes from the past floated behind her eyelids, like tendrils of fog drifting in from the lake. There were friends she'd had in elementary school, her high school prom, graduation from the university, her wedding day. The births of her daughters came sharply into focus, each birth different and yet the same.

"Such beautiful babies. They're beautiful girls," she murmured.

Were Jon and the girls okay? How long would her husband stay with his parents? In the future, would her daughters have their own beautiful babies—precious little ones she wouldn't be around to hold?

She fumbled in her purse to unearth a piece of paper and a pen, then struggled to find the right words. Scribbling on the page, she tried to read it in the dim light.

I'm sorry. It will be better for you this way. I love you.

The air was too warm inside the car. She grew drowsy. The paper drifted from her hand to the floor.

Dreamily she saw herself with Jon and the girls, dancing in a bright wildflower meadow. Nearby, a river wound its way through the lush countryside. High above them, a bald eagle circled, its sleek brown body silhouetted against fluffy cumulus clouds.

HOPE DOESN'T DISAPPOINT

From nowhere a large, aggressive mongrel dog charged into view. It chased her, howling and snapping, looking to leap onto her back. Its eyes were blinking multicolored lights, and its snarl made a noise like metallic music.

Cassie awakened with a start, her clothing damp with perspiration. Nausea overtook her, and she opened the car door and vomited into the gutter. She wiped her mouth with the back of her hand and lay back down in the seat, drifting back into the dark places of her dreams.

Constable Faris Halta and his partner Brian Appleton walked along the commercial downtown streets, alert for signs of trouble. At this time of night, their main calls were usually to break up fights outside the local bars and to coax homeless people to check into a shelter.

A cool wind had developed off the lake, and Faris and Brian picked up their pace. At Main and Carleton, the major intersection of Kettering's downtown core, they noticed a Honda Accord parked at the curb with a woman sprawled motionless in the front passenger seat.

Unable to rouse the woman with window knocking, Brian tried the passenger door. It was unlocked, and when he opened it, the woman's body slumped out the door toward him. Faris and Brian righted her, feeling for a pulse in her neck as they did so. The slow, regular beat told them she was alive. They shook her to try to wake her.

"What, what?" Groggy, she opened her eyes and stared at them.

"We're here to help you. What's your name?"

She opened her mouth to speak, closed her eyes, and slumped back in the seat.

Brian glanced at Faris. "What do you think? Another drunk, sleeping it off in her car?"

"I don't know. I don't smell any alcohol, and there aren't any open containers."

The acetaminophen bottle, along with a scrunched-up piece of paper, stood out as Faris ran his flashlight over the front seat area. He picked up the bottle, shook it, then opened it. Empty. Faris picked up the paper and handed it to Brian.

"There's some writing here. 'I'm sorry' is all I can make out." He held the flashlight closer as he struggled to see the words.

Faris radioed Dispatch and requested an ambulance. While they waited for the paramedics, Brian searched the back seat of the car. He found a garbage bag full of clothes, a plastic container with toiletries, and a lot of empty take-out containers.

"Looks like this woman's been living out of her car." He fished inside her purse and pulled out a wallet with a driver's license. He shined his flashlight on the license and held it up for Faris to see.

"Her name is Cassandra Alexis Bailey, date of birth December 12, 1980."

Brian had just returned the woman's wallet to her purse when the ambulance arrived. The pair gave the paramedics the details of their discovery and handed over the acetaminophen bottle, the scrunched-up note, and her purse. They watched silently as the attendants loaded Cassie into the ambulance and sped away, lights flashing and siren wailing.

Faris turned toward Brian, his face somber.

"I sure hope we found her in time."

HOPE DOESN'T DISAPPOINT

As soon as Cassie arrived at the hospital, she was bombarded with questions about what she took, how much, and what time she took it. Her brain felt like molasses. She couldn't remember and she didn't care. Her attempt at suicide was just something else she'd botched. After a lengthy stay in the emergency department, she was transferred to a bed on the tenth-floor psychiatric unit of the hospital. An IV pumped medication into her body to undo the effects of the pills.

Each hour in the hospital passed as a blur, and her emotions suffered along with her body. Whenever the lab technician came into her room to draw blood, Cassie didn't speak except to give rude answers. When nurses and doctors checked her liver, pressing on her abdomen, she swore at them. She screamed at them to leave her alone. It was as though another person had taken possession of her mind, a Cassie who was rebellious, venomous, suspicious.

Worthless.

Sedated, Cassie slept, unaware of Jon's presence. He'd arrived at the hospital later than he'd intended, but it was just as well, since he had no idea what to say to someone who had wanted to end their life only hours before.

She was thinner than he'd ever seen her. Her left arm lay outside the blanket, as marble-pale as if she'd crossed her suicide's finish line. He reached out to touch her hand, then stopped mid-motion. Her engagement ring was missing.

Hospital personnel had turned over all her valuables to him, but the ring hadn't been included. Someone had stolen it.

Maybe she pawned it.

The whisper snaked its way into his thoughts. Had she hocked—for money—one of the symbols that said to the world they're committed to each other?

Anger and despair boiled through him as he stared down at her still form. He wanted to shake her, punish her for trading their lives for her own entertainment. His hands were halfway to the bed when a quieter, sorrowful inner voice spoke to his heart.

Maybe she pawned it to stay alive, not to gamble.

Maybe she pawned it to try and do better.

Maybe she tried to die because she thought you'd never let her come home.

He dropped into the chair, a wave of horror and remorse drowning him. His heart thumped against the walls of his chest, hammering in agony. Cold sweat ran down the sides of his face.

He himself could have been the reason she wanted to die. If the constables hadn't found her, she might have succeeded. Their girls would be without the mother they loved. Without the woman he loved more than any other. And it would have been his fault.

Jon bowed his head to pray.

"God in Heaven, please let Cassie live through this. She's the most important person in my life and our children's lives. Maybe I was responsible for her doing what she did—I hope not— but please give me the chance to tell her I'm sorry for anything I did to hurt her." He stopped. His throat closed, and tears threatened to choke him. "I'm being selfish, Lord, but I can't help it. Please. Let her live."

He gulped deep breaths and grew calmer. He sat back in the chair in the night's silence and after a long moment heard—or thought he heard—words spoken on the air.

Twenty-nine words.

HOPE DOESN'T DISAPPOINT

I am the resurrection and the life; he who believes in me, though he die, yet shall he live, and whoever lives and believes in me shall never die.

He stumbled out of the room and down the corridor to a deserted waiting room. He sat doubled over, his rasping sobs echoing in the dark.

After a time, he quieted. What he'd heard weren't words of reproach. They were Jesus's words—words of comfort and hope, words of life. Jesus would give Cassie strength to get through this. To him, Jesus would give the courage to face whatever might lie ahead

On the morning of the fourth day, Cassie woke to footsteps.

Jon and the girls tiptoed in. It was the first time the girls had seen their mom. The three of them approached her and stood solemnly in a semicircle. She stared back at them.

"You don't look so good, Mom." Anne-Marie said. "What happened?"

"I ... uh ... took too much medicine."

"Why?" Jesse's voice was plaintive. She walked over to the bed, perched on the edge, and reached to touch her mother's face.

Several seconds passed before Cassie answered.

"It was a foolish thing to do." Wanting to change the subject, she stretched out her arms. "Can I have a hug?"

Awkwardly, Jesse gave Cassie a hug and kiss. Anne-Marie came over and joined the two. She pulled them closer and breathed in the scent of their hair.

"I've missed you guys so much."

Tears welled in Anne-Marie's eyes. "We've missed you too. When are you coming home?"

Cassie glanced at Jon.

"Your mother and I will talk about that," Jon said. He looked thoughtful. "Do me a favor?"

"Sure, Dad," Jesse said. "What?"

"There's a cafeteria on the first floor. Could you two get me a cup of coffee?" Jon pulled a ten-dollar bill out of his pocket and handed it to Jesse. "Use the change to buy yourselves something. Would you like some tea, Cassie?"

She shook her head.

Jesse waved the ten-dollar bill. "Let's go, Anne-Marie. They want to talk grown-up stuff." She beelined for the door. "Maybe the cafeteria will have donuts."

"Or pastries." The sisters jostled each other to get out the door. Once they were gone, Jon pulled his chair to Cassie's bed and sat down.

"When do you think they'll let you go?"

Cassie sighed. "They want to do a psychiatric assessment before discharging me. I wish I could go today." She stared at the far wall. "Maybe the fact I'm already hooked up with a mental health group will help speed things up."

Jon reached out and took Cassie's hand. "Can you talk about it?" He stroked her fingers. "Can you tell me why?"

Cassie pulled her hand away. Straightening the sheets and the blanket had taken on sudden importance. She tried unsuccessfully to smooth out all the wrinkles while her eyes burned with hot unshed tears.

"I've been living out of my car. I'd finally saved up enough money for the first and last month's rent for an apartment." She took a deep breath. "I gambled it away. When I asked Dad to loan me the money, he refused." Sobs shook her. "And you told me I can't come home until I quit gambling. I—"

She stopped crying long enough to take in a gulp of air. "I don't seem to be able to break away from it, Jon. If I can't stop gambling, and I can't be with my family, there's no reason to carry on." She sank down lower in the bed and wept into a crumpled handful of bedsheet.

Jon bent down and brushed his fingers against her face. "I need to tell you something."

She uncovered her face and looked up. "What? You want a divorce?"

He dropped to his knees on the floor and took both her hands in his. "No, no, nothing like that." He gazed at her for a long moment, then looked down. "I'm sorry for making you think you couldn't come home again. It was wrong of me to say anything that made you feel that way, and I hope you can find it in your heart to forgive me."

She was silent. He'd been so adamant, so final about her not coming home until she didn't gamble anymore. At least now he saw what an awful effect his words had had on her.

He looked up again at her face. She nodded.

"You're forgiven." She poked at a wrinkle in the blanket and sniffled. After a long moment she said, "Can I come home?"

"Yes. We'll take it a day at a time and see how things go. I'll look for an apartment or a house to rent." He glanced away. "We're still living with my parents."

He looked out the window, then back at her. "Cass, have you considered praying for help with the gambling? Jesus can help you more than anything anyone else can offer. I'm sure of it."

She shook her head. "I don't want a crutch. You know I've always handled things myself."

He gave her a faint smile. "How's that working for you so far?"

She grimaced.

"I'm sorry. I shouldn't have said that."

"I can't make any promises, Jon. But I want to come home." She picked at a fingernail. "And I apologize for what I said to you in the diner."

"You were upset. Besides, I don't even remember exactly what you said."

I don't deserve this man.

Shame ate at her, and her cheeks burned with it. She reached for him, wanting the feel of his arms around her, just as footsteps thumped down the hallway.

Jon gave her a wry smile and kissed her forehead. "The girls are back."

Anne-Marie and Jesse bounded into the room, spilling some of Jon's coffee as they waved a brown paper bag.

"We got pastries," Jesse said. "Want one?"

Jon and Cassie shook their heads. Jon held out his hands. "Give me the coffee before you spill it all."

Anne-Marie handed the Styrofoam cup to her father along with his change. She pulled out a pastry for Jesse and one for herself. Cassie couldn't help smiling as she watched them eat.

"I'm coming home when they spring me out of here."

The girls ran and kissed her, smearing her face with their own red-jelly-and-sugar-glazed ones. Then they sat on the edge of her bed to finish their treats.

"Goody!" Jesse exclaimed. She looked at her father. "Can we get our own place now, so we don't have to live at Grandma and Grandpa's anymore?"

"We can." He watched the two take the last bites of their goodies. "Are you done?"

They nodded, and he stood. "Time to go, then. We don't want to exhaust your mother."

"Seeing the three of you doesn't tire me," Cassie said, as she dabbed jelly and sugar off her cheeks and touched a suspiciously sticky strand of hair near her face. "Not at all."

HOPE DOESN'T DISAPPOINT

Jon gazed at her. "I can tell from looking at you. We've worn you out. Don't worry. We'll be back."

The girls kissed their mom and walked out into the hallway. Jon pecked his wife on the cheek. "After we get back to my parents, I'll ask my dad to drive me over to get your car. Where is it again?"

"If the constables haven't moved it, it's near the corner of Main and Carleton."

"Is that where the police found you?"

She nodded.

"Thank God they found you in time." Jon moved to the door, then turned, a pained expression in his eyes. "My life would never be the same without you."

Cassie hung her head. "I didn't think anybody cared."

"I care because I love you."

Raising her head, Casssie peered into Jon's eyes, "Don't ever stop."

Jon shook his head. "I won't."

A full minute passed before either of them spoke. "Let me know when they're ready to discharge you."

"I will."

On the dot of seven-thirty, Deva Ramsaran bustled into Cassie's room, carrying a large satchel made of woven bamboo with brightly colored crocheted flowers on the sides. Deva leaned down to the bed and gave her a tight hug.

"I've been praying for you, lovey."

"How did you know I was here?"

"Well now, after you missed your shift at work, and I couldn't reach you, I was prayin' and fellowshippin' with the Lord. He told me to hustle down to the General because you were hurtin' in here. Have you been in an accident or somethin'?"

Cassie shook her head.

"That's good."

Deva removed some takeout containers from her bamboo bag. "I brought you some treats."

Cassie peeked inside each one in turn—a piece of Deva's delicious strawberry cheesecake rested in one, a homemade muffin in another one. A fresh garden salad filled one more, along with a small container of Cassie's favorite dressing.

Deva smiled, a mischievous look in her eye. "Just in case they aren't feedin' you right in here."

"You're one of a kind, Deva." Warmth filled Cassie's heart.

"I'm not finished yet." The older woman reached to the bottom of the bag. "I brought you some shower gel and body lotion to make you feel nice when you take a shower before you get out of here." Deva positioned the bottles on the bedside stand and studied Cassie. "When are you getting out of here?"

"Maybe tomorrow."

"Why are you in here?"

"I took too much medicine."

"On purpose?"

Cassie nodded.

Deva tsked, but her expression didn't change. "Whatever's goin' on in your life must be pretty bad."

"I have an addiction, Deva. I've just got to pick myself up by the bootstraps and get over it."

Her friend shook her head. "That ain't gonna work, honey. The harder you try, the more you're just gonna fail."

"That's not very encouraging."

"Oh, sweetie, you want encouragement? I got just the thing for you. If you look in the Gospels in the New

Testament, you'll never find a place where Jesus turned anybody away, anybody who reached out to him for healing or deliverance. Jesus came to set the captives free."

Cassie couldn't help smiling. "You're the second person who's told me that today."

"God doesn't give up on us, dearie. The Book of Revelation says Jesus is knockin' at the door of our hearts, just waitin' for us to open that door so he can come in and fellowship with us. Doesn't that sound good—communin' with Jesus?"

Cassie massaged her temples. "It's a lot to think about, Deva."

"Well, my advice is don't think too long, girlie. Otherwise, you're missin' out on all the joy and freedom Jesus is offerin' you." She paused. "Are ya comin' back to work?"

"If you'll have me."

Deva reached down and folded Cassie in her arms.

"I'll always have ya," she whispered in Cassie's ear, "just like Jesus always says welcome back when we repent, no matter what we've done."

She kissed Deva's cheek as the old woman's tears mingled with her own.

CHAPTER TWENTY-NINE

During the winter months, to keep trim and fit, Ben and Maddie joined a fitness center located midway between their two residences. At least one evening per week, they met either to swim in the pool or work out on the machines. On this particular evening, they played racquetball.

After the game and showering in the locker rooms, Ben placed two smoothies on a large, glass-topped coffee table in the center's conversation zone. Although it was only nine-thirty in the evening, few patrons made use of the area.

"We have the place more or less to ourselves," Ben observed as they sat down on one of the sofas surrounding the table.

Maddie nodded and watched him take a sip of his drink.

"Busy day with the pediatricians and kids?"

"Nonstop." Maddie shrugged. "The usual meltdowns, messes to clean up, and worried parents. How was yours?"

"One of the members of my group for addicted gamblers is in the hospital." Ben rubbed his forehead, eyes troubled. "A suicide attempt." He stared at the far wall before continuing. "It doesn't happen all that often with my clients, but when it does, I feel like I've failed them. I keep asking myself what I could have said or done differently."

Maddie reached over and took his hand. "What could you have done to bring about a different outcome?"

Ben sighed. "Spent more time talking individually after group? Provided a referral to see someone privately on a weekly basis?" Ben shook his head. "I sensed the person was struggling and not being honest about their gambling. I should have listened to my gut."

"I believe the people we work with need Jesus."

"They do." Ben looked thoughtful. "Will you trust God with me for her salvation and deliverance from gambling?"

"Of course, I will." Maddie looked down at their hands. "And Ben, don't beat yourself up over what happened. Ultimately each person is responsible for their own lives."

"I know. Thanks for reminding me." He gave her a peck on the cheek. "Sometimes the therapist needs a therapist."

Maddie smiled. "Anytime."

CHAPTER THIRTY

"Jon, I feel like I'm walking on eggs. Whenever I've been out, you ask me where I've been and what I've done." Cassie looked down. "I know I haven't been a trustworthy person, and I get where you're coming from, but your constant questions rattle me."

They were in their first appointment with Honey Ritchie, a well-groomed middle-aged Christian marriage and family therapist Ben had recommended. Cassie sat on one of the office's two loveseats, Jon on the other. Honey settled on her chair between the two.

"Jon, what's your response to what Cassie just said?"

Seconds ticked by before he spoke.

"I have problems trusting her. I don't want our world to fall apart again right under my nose."

"I get it," Cassie shot back before Honey could respond. "But do you have to check my internet search history and the bank balances, including mine, five times a day?"

Honey interjected. "Cassie, why do you think Jon does the things you just mentioned?"

"Like I said, I get it. He doesn't want me jeopardizing our family again."

Jon rubbed his hand over the arm of the loveseat.

"Cassie, it's because of fear and embarrassment I do those things. Fear your gambling will put us at risk again, and embarrassment because I should have been aware of the extent of your gambling. If I'd found out the magnitude of the problem, I could have stepped in sooner." He glanced down at his shoes. "I guess now I want to be proactive rather than reactive."

Jon had found his family a house to rent, not far from their previous address. He'd been more than fair. Still, Cassie was irked.

"If you want to know the truth, all the checking up you do makes me want to gamble more." She stopped, and her eyes welled with tears. "And I'm afraid too. I'm fearful I'll mess up and you'll ask me to leave. The thought of having to leave you and the girls again—the thought just kills me."

It almost did, once. The unspoken thought hung in the sudden silence.

Honey looked from Cassie to Jon. "It's going to take time for you two to build trust in each other. What are a few things you could do to start building trust again?

Several minutes passed before Cassie spoke.

"Don't expect too much too soon."

Jon grimaced. "Yeah. I know I need to develop patience."

Cassie smiled. "Remember that whole summer we painted houses together? You kept telling me, 'Hurry up. Hurry up.' I heard that phrase in my dreams." She stopped and looked at her hands before looking back at Jon. "I need to go at my own pace."

Jon rubbed his forehead. "I'm coming to realize that."

"What's another suggestion?"

"Admitting our mistakes. I need to acknowledge when I do something that shows Cassie I don't trust her."

"Is that an easy thing for you to do?"

"No, but I'm willing to work on it."

"What else?" Honey asked.

"Put the past in the past." Cassie glanced at Jon. "That's a hard one for both of us.

"It is."

"In order not to dwell on the past, it's important to remember you can't change it. But you can change the future." Honey glanced at Jon and Cassie and then down at her notes. When she looked up at them again, she held up her hand and counted off on her fingers.

"One, don't expect too much too soon. Two, admit mistakes. And three, put the past in the past. Those are three great suggestions. Do you have some practical ideas for developing your trust in each other?"

"I have one suggestion that might help." Cassie glanced at her husband. "I don't mind if I don't have access to our main bank account. But I would appreciate it if he didn't check my personal bank account. I want to take responsibility for it."

"What do you think, Jon?"

He thought for a moment. "That sounds fair. Change your password so I don't have access."

Cassie felt a smile tug at her lips. They were making progress.

Honey made a note in their file. "What else can you do?"

"Well, maybe Cassie and I could sit down together once a month to discuss where we are financially. That way, even though she can't get into the main bank account, she'll know how we're doing."

"That's good," Cassie responded.

"What else?"

"We don't have credit cards anymore," Cassie said. "But I'd like to set up a debit card for my personal bank account. That way I don't have to carry around cash all the time."

Jon nodded. "I'm okay with that. It makes sense."

Cassie felt encouraged enough to bring up another sticking point.

"It really bothers me you check my online search history all the time."

Jon stared at her. "You know why."

"Yeah. To see if I've been on online gambling sites."

He shrugged and looked at Honey. "I'm not sure what to do about that. She feels I'm violating her privacy, but I have to know if she's gambling online to hold her accountable."

Honey tapped her notes with her pen. "There are apps you can download through your bank to block a bank account from being used online—for gambling transactions, for instance."

"Would you agree to putting a block on your bank account, Cassie?" Jon asked.

She hung her head. "I'm ashamed I would have to do something like that. But I guess anything that puts an obstacle in the way of my gambling is good."

"So, you'll put the block on?"

She nodded.

The counselor cleared her throat. "Cassie, there's a word you just said I want to pick up on. You said you feel ashamed. What role do you think shame plays in your life?"

If only I didn't have to be here.

Focusing her eyes on the floor, Cassie didn't respond. Jon shifted uncomfortably on the loveseat.

"Cassie?"

She lifted her head and a tear slipped down her cheek. "I feel so unworthy, so worthless. That word goes round and round on a loop in my head."

"What are you unworthy of?"

She opened her mouth to speak but nothing came out. Nearly a minute passed before she managed to whisper, "Love."

With a pained look on his face, Jon got up and sat beside her. He put his arm around her and held her close.

"Why do you feel you're unworthy of love?" Honey's question showed Cassie she wasn't going to let the matter go. Cassie squirmed.

"My dad used to tell me I was no good, and that I'd turn out just like my mom."

"And have you turned out like your mom?"

"In a way, yes. She drank alcohol to excess. I gamble to excess."

"Remember you always have a choice. Whenever that urge to gamble intensifies, there are techniques you can use to wait it out until it begins to subside. I think you're aware of some of them."

Cassie nodded.

Honey gave her a big smile. "And it looks to me that at least one person loves you."

Turning her tear-stained face to Jon, Cassie kissed him on the cheek. "I love you," she choked.

Jon gave his wife a tight hug. "I love you too. Never forget that."

Honey allowed a long minute to pass before she spoke again.

"How does it make you feel when you hear Jon say he loves you?"

"It makes me feel conflicted. I want his love. I need his love. But because of what I've done, I find it hard to believe he does love me."

"You're having problems believing his love for you?"

"Yes."

"As the saying goes, actions speak louder than words. Do you think Jon's actions show he loves you?"

Cassie glanced at the floor before looking up at Honey. "They do. He should have written me off as a lost cause a long time ago, but he didn't."

"I couldn't write you off," Jon said. "Number one, you weren't—and aren't—a lost cause. Second is what I believe in my heart about Jesus."

Cassie looked at him, puzzlement on her face.

"Jesus could have written off humanity, but he didn't," Jon said. "He voluntarily paid a terrible price to buy us back from Satan and allow us a relationship with God." He gave Cassie a wry smile. "If Jesus was willing to suffer and die for every man, woman, and child on earth, no matter what they'd done—well, who am I to call you a lost cause?"

Honey nodded. "I agree. To me, the courage and love of Jesus are irresistible."

Cassie had to admit the deepest longing of her heart was to be loved, not with strings attached, but unconditionally. But did Jesus really offer that kind of love? Did anyone?

"Our time is almost over," Honey said. "I like to close every marriage session with positive affirmations. Jon, I'd like you to tell Cassie one thing you appreciate about her, and Cassie, I'd like you to do the same for Jon."

Cassie stared at her feet before looking up at her husband.

"I value the fact you haven't given up on me. That means a great deal."

His gaze met and held hers. "I appreciate your courage, Cass"—his voice caught, and he cleared his throat—"and your determination to keep going."

She reached for his hand and squeezed it.

Honey tilted her head and smiled. "How does it feel to hear those words from each other?"

"Good." They both spoke in unison and then laughed.

"A gentle reminder, you two. You don't have to be in my office to affirm each other. You can do it anytime, anywhere."

"Why is it always easier to concentrate on the negative rather than the positive?" Cassie asked.

"That's the way we're wired. We default to the negative. We have to put effort into developing the positive."

Honey glanced down at her notes. "I have some homework for you. There's two parts to it. The first part is I want you to tell me how many times each day over the next week you say something affirming to each other. And I don't want it to be a guess. Keep a record. The second part is to write down the one affirmation your spouse made during the week that stood out the most for you. Clear?"

Jon and Cassie nodded.

Two days later, Jon and Daniel sat in a back booth at their favorite coffee shop, Jon with yogurt and coffee and Daniel with a donut and tea.

"Dan, the thing I'm really struggling with now is fear. Trusting Cassie again is a huge challenge." Jon hung his head. Seconds passed before he raised it and looked at his friend. "Even though we're seeing a marriage therapist to get some help, having confidence in her honesty is a big issue for me."

"I can imagine. I think your trust in each other will build over time." Dan sipped his tea. "You mentioned fear. Where do you think fear comes from?"

Jon's mind flashed to the night he received the call from the hospital and arrived to learn she'd tried to commit suicide. That night was engraved forever in his brain. Fear had gurgled in his stomach like an underground spring, almost tangible. How was it possible? Was he responsible in some way? How could he cope with the reality of it all?

Jon had difficulty shaking the recollection. It took several seconds for him to realize Dan was waiting for an answer.

"From Satan, I guess."

"You're right. It's from Satan. But remember. Who defeated Satan?"

Jon gave him a blank stare. "Jesus?"

"Absolutely right. Jesus conquered Satan—and fear—when he rose from the dead."

"So what should I do when I feel like I'm drowning in fear? Pray?"

"Don't give in to the fear. Tell it to leave you. Tell it out loud. Tell the fear it has no dominion over you because of Jesus's sacrifice. Doesn't matter if you need to do it every twenty seconds. Keep at it until the fear obeys and retreats." He held up a forefinger for emphasis. "And it will obey you and retreat, because it knows the name of Jesus."

Dan took a bite of his donut. "Want a piece? It's delicious." He pushed his plate across the table, offering. Jon shook his head.

"Remember," Daniel said, "in every situation, we have a choice. On one side, there's God and what he says. On the other, there's Satan and what he says. We can either listen to the lies of Satan, or we can stand on the truth of what God says."

Jon took a bite of yogurt and nodded at his colleague. "Thanks, Dan. I'm learning a lot."

Daniel smiled. "You're just beginning, Jon. Learning about God and the truth of his word is a lifelong process."

"Well, I'm in for the long haul."

CHAPTER THIRTY-ONE

Cassie had many errands to run, and she needed to get them done before 11:00 a.m. so she could get to work by 11:30. One of the servers had called in sick, and Deva needed her at the restaurant by 11:30 at the latest. As she headed to her car, the warmth in the atmosphere and beautiful blue skies made her glad spring had arrived. Lilac blooms infused the air with their strong, heady scent. She breathed in their perfume and hummed a little tune. Their last session with the marriage therapist had gone well, and she felt she and Jon were making progress. She also hadn't gambled for over two weeks.

Her first stop was the dry cleaners to pick up one of Jon's suits and his shirts for the week. When she got inside the shop, a long line greeted her. The line moved slowly as molasses in winter, and she shifted impatiently from foot to foot as she waited for her turn. When she finally got to the front of the line, the attendant informed her Jon's shirts were ready but not the suit. Now she had to make an extra trip to come back for it.

At the grocery store, things weren't much better. She hadn't made a list and couldn't remember all the items she needed. When she got to the checkout line, the woman in front of her pulled a newspaper flyer out of her purse and started doing price comparisons, making sure she got the lowest cost on her purchases. Cassie eyed the other lanes, meaning to get into a shorter line, but each lane overflowed with people whose grocery carts were filled to the brim.

Muttering under her breath, she finally loaded her items onto the conveyor belt, setting each one down with a bang. By the time the lady finished her price comparison and purchase and Cassie reached the cashier, her head was ready to explode.

"That shouldn't be allowed."

"What, ma'am?"

"Comparison shopping. It slows down the line. I've got less than thirty minutes to get to work."

"But by matching prices, the store stays competitive."

Cassie could feel her cheeks heating up. "Are you saying you agree with the policy?"

The cashier looked at Cassie like she had six heads. "I'm not saying I agree or disagree. I'm just telling you why the store allows it." The woman hesitated before adding, "In fact, it encourages it."

"C'mon, lady. Quit the chitchat. You're holding up the line."

The short, balding gentleman behind Cassie glared at her through frameless round glasses, making his hazel-colored eyes appear larger than they were. "We're all in a hurry here."

Piqued, Cassie scowled back. "If the store didn't have this policy, we wouldn't get held up by someone wanting to save a few pennies."

"A penny saved is a penny earned."

Turning her back to the man with his worn-out adage, Cassie waited as the cashier rang through her last purchase. She paid for her merchandise, bagged her items quickly, and marched out of the store. In the future, she'd shop somewhere else. Angry bile filled her mouth and she swallowed it down with a gulp. She had a bare ten minutes to get to the jewelry store for a new watch battery.

On the way to the retailer, she passed the casino. She turned her head away, doing her best to ignore it. "Keep going, Cassie, keep going," she chided herself. "You've been doing good."

At the jeweler's, she smiled when she stepped inside and saw only the owner and an elderly lady with a blue rinse on her hair.

When my hair goes white, I most certainly will not color it blue.

The lady had come in with a walker which was parked off to one side. She leaned heavily on the counter while the jeweler brought various pairs of earrings out of the display case for her to examine. In order not to intrude, Cassie went to the other side of the store and looked down at all the beautiful items.

"These are silver earrings with a white opal."

"They're nice, but I'm allergic to silver studs. I need gold ones."

The woman had a high-pitched, whiny voice. Her tone grated on Cassie's already taut nerves.

Cassie could hear the jeweler opening a showcase.

"I have these in 14 karat gold as well."

A few seconds passed before the woman responded. In her mind's eye, Cassie could see the lady turning the earrings over in her veined hands. "They're pretty. How much?"

"Nine hundred seventy-five dollars."

The woman tsked. "Way more than I want to spend."

Cassie knew she couldn't wait any longer. She was just about to leave when a younger lady walked into the store and spoke to the elderly woman.

"Time to go, Mom. You'll have to buy your earrings another day." Cassie kept her back to the two women but heard them walking toward the door, the walker's wheels squeaking across the floor.

Just as she turned around to speak to the jeweler, the store's Muzak system came on, playing "Shape of My Heart" by Sting. One of the restaurants in the casino played the tune often. Cassie's heartbeat picked up, and the reminder of the casino and the comfort it brought her enveloped her like the feel of a newborn baby snuggled against her chest. Passing the casino and then hearing one of the songs she often heard there were irresistible. She had to go.

Don't go, Cassie. You've been doing so well.

She thrust the thought aside. The pull was too great. Then she remembered the last time she'd gambled, she'd lost most of the cash she'd saved. She needed more money. But where could she get it?

As the mother and daughter left the store, the telephone rang. The proprietor hurried into another room to answer it, leaving the opal earrings on the black jewelry display tray. Cassie glanced around the store, noting the cameras focused on the jewelry cases. She moved closer to the earrings. All she had to do was move the tray out of the camera's range, pick up the earrings quickly, and walk unhurriedly out of the store. She moved closer, listening while the jeweler continued in what appeared to be a long, involved conversation.

So easy. You can be long gone before he comes back. And he can't really identify you because you had your back to him most of the time.

She moved the tray toward her. The opal earrings lay in front of her. She reached out her hand. One small scoop with her fingers and they'd be hers. What had the jeweler said they were worth—nine seventy-five? She could sell them on the internet. Then she'd have money for gambling. Her fingers had nearly closed around the earrings when she stopped. Heat spread through her body from the depths of her stomach to the top of her head. She was inches from turning into a common thief. How had she stooped this low?

Uttering a low cry, she fled the store. Once inside her car, she lowered her head on the steering wheel. "What have I become?" she moaned.

What have I become?

CHAPTER THIRTY-TWO

Cassie knelt beside their bed, sobbing as Jon paced back and forth in the small chamber like a tiger in a cage.

"At least I told you. And I didn't have much money with me anyway."

Jon sat down at the bottom of the mattress. "You work hard for your money. How could you blow it away just like that?" He snapped his fingers, startling her. She jumped and buried her face in the bedcovers.

"Why, Cassie?"

She groaned. "I can't stay away." The bedding muffled her words. "I can't explain it. It's … it's like a trumpet, a voice, calling me."

Jon shook his head, stood to his feet, and padded out and down the hall.

Climbing into bed, Cassie stared at the ceiling.

"Is there no hope?" she murmured. "We're attending marriage counseling. I haven't missed any group sessions. And I still give in to the urge."

She tried to get comfortable, but sleep would not come. Giving up, she got up and went to the washroom. A light shone underneath the slightly open door of the bedroom they used as an office. She pushed it open and saw Jon with his arms folded on his desk and his head on top. He was talking, but his voice was muffled by his arms. She strained to hear.

"God, I'm coming to you for Cassie." His voice was raw. "Show her who you are. She needs you more than she knows."

She stepped farther into the room, and he looked up at the sound. His eyes were bloodshot.

"Are you all right?"

He nodded, his gaze focused on her. Several seconds passed before he spoke.

"Can I pray for you, Cassie?"

"Why?"

"Because I don't think you'll do it for yourself."

She remembered the peace she'd felt when Deva prayed for her. "All right." She pulled over the chair from her desk, and they sat facing each other. Jon reached out and took her hands in his own.

"Father God, you love Cassie and me more than we can ever comprehend. You love us no matter what we've done. You know Cassie is struggling with this addiction, and you know her heart. My prayer is she will come to know you and your heart, your love for her. I pray she will let you carry the burden, and free her. I pray this in the precious name of your Son, Jesus. Amen."

Silently, Jon stood to his feet and pulled her up. Without saying a word, he led her back to their bedroom. Together they lay down, and Jon put his arm around Cassie and held her close. His warmth permeated her body and spread into her soul. The tightness in her chest lessened, and she closed her eyes. Just about to drift off to sleep, she heard Jon murmur, "Father, may Cassie come to know that underneath her are your powerful, everlasting, almighty arms, stretched out and ready to catch her."

HOPE DOESN'T DISAPPOINT

Within minutes he was snoring. She turned and put her arm around his chest.

"Love, Jon. That's what I need the most." She breathed along with the rhythm of his breath. "Unconditional love, with no strings attached."

CHAPTER THIRTY-THREE

Surprisingly, the middle of June was cool. It rained a lot and the dismal weather conditions did nothing to brighten Cassie's spirits. The days she managed to stay away from the casino were good days, and the days she gave in to the urge to gamble were terrible. She and Jon continued to see the marriage therapist, and Cassie regularly attended Ben Gallagher's group meetings.

One day after a group session, as she walked by Ben on her way to the exit, he commented, "You look tired, Cassie. I see dark circles around your eyes. Trouble sleeping?"

Cassie nodded.

"Want to talk about it?"

There was no way she wanted to discuss it. She headed for the door, then she hesitated and turned back to Ben. She needed all the support she could get.

"I might as well be honest. I haven't stopped gambling." Defeated, she looked to find disappointment on Ben's face, but she saw none.

"It's not uncommon for people with a gambling addiction to relapse after they begin treatment. In fact, many experts see relapse as part of the recovery journey."

"I don't want a journey, Ben. I want it finished now."

"I'm not saying it can't happen overnight. It could, but more often it's a process." Seconds passed before Ben spoke again. "What kind of support do you have outside the group?"

Cassie thought a minute.

"I'd have to say my two main supports are my husband and my boss." She frowned. "The only problem with those two is they're always telling me I need Jesus and to read the Bible."

Ben grinned. "Maybe you should listen to them."

"Yeah."

Not you too.

She glanced at her watch. "I've got to go now. The girls will be home from school soon. Thanks for listening."

Ben nodded. Cassie made a hasty retreat for the door. She didn't want Ben digging too deeply.

CHAPTER THIRTY-FOUR

Jon didn't get the computer monitor turned off in time and now Cassie stood behind him. It was Saturday afternoon, and the girls had gone to a friend's house to play. Cassie had been downstairs doing laundry, and it seemed Jon hadn't heard her come into their bedroom office.

Her eyes narrowed as she peered at the screen. "Are you looking at my online search history?

Jon kept quiet.

"You are, aren't you? Didn't you say in one of our therapy sessions you'd work on not doing that?"

Jon mumbled something under his breath.

"Trust, Jon that's what we're trying to develop here. Remember?"

She paced up and down behind him. "This means you still don't trust me."

"It's not that I don't trust you. I just like to check every so often."

Cassie put her hands on her hips.

"Admit it. You're afraid I'm going to embarrass you again. I know some of your buddies found out about the foreclosure back when it happened, and they haven't been so quick to invite you out with them anymore. They're wondering what's happened to good old true-blue Jonathan Bailey."

She ground her teeth. She knew Jon could hear it.

"Oh, and I should add true-blue Christian Jonathan Bailey. How could a real man—a real Christian man—let his wife gamble so much they lost their house? Is that what your friends are saying?

Jon hung his head.

"The guy who's supposed to be in control all the time, isn't."

"Look, Cassie. I feel I failed you and the girls by not dealing with the problem sooner."

"And now I'm your little problem who has to be 'dealt with.'" Her fingers sketched quotation marks in the air around the words 'dealt with.'

"Stop it." Jon's voice increased half a decibel. He took a deep breath to calm himself. "You're putting words in my mouth."

"I know you see me as a problem, just like my dad did."

"I'm not your dad. I'm your husband. I wish you'd get that through your head."

"Sometimes I can't tell the difference." Her voice changed to a gruff imitation of a male voice. "What's the matter with you, Cassie? Why can't you get your act together, Cassie? You'll never amount to much, Cassie.'"

"I don't say those things to you."

"You don't have to. Your actions say them for you."

Their chairs were now facing each other. Opposite each other.

"All I'm trying to do is keep everything together," he said. "Not let our lives descend into chaos again. Can you understand that?'

"Oh, yeah, I understand."

"No, you don't." Jon raised his hands in frustration.

"I do." She got up from her chair so fast it tipped over and bounced. "See you later, Goody Two Shoes."

She kicked the chair back, narrowly missing Jon, and flew out the door. The floor creaked as she stomped down the hall.

Jon rose from his chair and called after her.

"Where are you going? To gamble away money we don't have?"

Seconds later, the front door slammed shut.

Jon and Dan ate their bag lunches in Jon's office, spreading their goodies out in front of them. The smell of Dan's garlicky Italian meatballs filled the air, making Jon's nose twitch. Out on the floor, the showroom hummed. Jon could see the sales reps writing up orders. Hopefully this would be a good month.

He took a sip from his Styrofoam coffee cup and cleared his throat. "Things aren't going well between Cassie and me. We're fighting a lot."

Dan nodded and waited quietly for Jon to continue.

"Cassie takes offense at everything I say. And she's so resistant to hearing anything about Jesus." He looked down at the table. "Sometimes I don't know what to do."

"Keep loving her, Jon. More than anything, she needs your unconditional love."

"It isn't easy. She can be pretty nasty."

"Don't forget. It takes two to tango. "

Jon hung his head. Several seconds passed before he spoke. "You're right. I guess I can be pretty spiteful sometimes."

Dan poked at a meatball and spoke without looking at Jon. "Satan's good at putting blinders over people's eyes, and the more they fight and argue and hurt each other, the better he likes it. And pride?" He waved an arm in an expansive gesture. "Don't even get me started. Proverbs says pride goes before destruction and haughtiness before a fall. You really have to watch out for that."

"Pride? Me?" Jon shot Dan an incredulous look. "Well, I mean, sometimes it's a temptation to think I'm better than Cassie, but I'm not."

Dan gave him a rueful smile. "There go all of us but for the grace of God."

The two men sat quietly, each lost in thought.

"Don't despair," Dan said, "about Cassie accepting Jesus as her Savior. In the parable of the lost sheep, Jesus asked if a man who owned a hundred sheep wouldn't leave the ninety-nine and go after the one who wandered off. The answer of course, is yes, he would. God has his ways of bringing his lost lambs home."

CHAPTER THIRTY-FIVE

Anne-Marie and Jesse, each carrying a glass of milk, sat down across from their parents at the kitchen table. For their bedtime snack, Cassie placed a plate of crackers and cheese and plump green grapes in the middle.

Jon stirred some sugar into his coffee, his spoon tinkling against the ceramic mug. Frowning, Cassie put her hand on his arm to stop him from banging the spoon. She faced the girls and waved her hand dismissively at her husband.

"Your dad has some announcement he wants to make."

"What is it?" Jesse moved restlessly on her chair. Grabbing some crackers and cheese, she took a bite. "M-m-m, I like this cheese. What kind is it?" She took another mouthful, cracker crumbs all over her lips and pajama top.

"Havarti."

"Buy some more, Mom. It's good."

"I have more reading to do before I get into bed." Anne-Marie's face was glum.

Jon frowned. "This won't take long, girls, so don't get your tails into a knot."

Anne-Marie rolled her eyes. Jesse scowled.

"Are we moving back to our old house?" Jesse looked hopeful, but Cassie shook her head.

"Maybe in time we'll be able to buy another house, but not right now." Folding her hands on the table, she looked at each daughter.

Might as well take the plunge now.

She swallowed hard. "You've brought up our old house, so I guess tonight is as good a time as any to tell you. You've both known something's been wrong, but not exactly what. Am I right?"

Anne-Marie focused her eyes on the table. "At school, we've been learning people can be sick in their heads as well as in their bodies. I thought maybe your brain was sick."

"I didn't know what the matter was." Jesse's eyes brimmed with tears. "I was afraid you were going to die because of some disease you had."

"Our family has gotten into financial trouble because I've been gambling."

"You mean like playing the lottery? My friend at school, Tamara—her mother won ten thousand dollars and her family took a trip to Disney World. If you won the lottery, maybe we could take a trip." Anne-Marie's eyes glinted in the light from the overhead fixture.

"No, not the lottery. I've been playing the slot machines at the casino and gambling online. Sometimes you win money and sometimes you lose."

A lot.

"Oh. That kind of gambling."

She found it difficult to look at the disappointment in her children's eyes. It was a shadow of the condemnation she had seen so often on her dad's face. Not wanting to dwell on the thought, she added hastily, "But I'm getting help to quit."

"And it's our fault you two didn't know what was happening." Jon looked crestfallen. "I think we were afraid to tell you the truth." Thinking a minute, he added, "Or maybe we were ashamed to tell you why our family has been in jeopardy."

Jesse whipped her phone from her pocket, brought up a website and typed something into it. "Jeopardy means danger." She spoke authoritatively, glancing at Anne-Marie to make sure her older sister had heard.

"I know what it means, smarty pants." Anne-Marie retorted. "And I can look words up on my phone just as fast as you can."

Cassie gave the girls her firm stop it now stare.

Jesse finished her milk and began moving the glass around the table.

"Are we just going to talk about bad things?" As she continued to fiddle, she nearly knocked the tumbler over, causing Jon to frown. When her father put his hand on her arm, she stopped.

"Getting back to my announcement, what I wanted to tell you," he said, "is I'm going to start taking you girls to church."

The girls froze, but only for a second. Anne-Marie spoke first. "I don't want to go to church."

"I don't want to go either." Jesse lifted her chin, a defiant look on her face.

Cassie kept quiet. She had no intention of attending church.

"Is it okay with you if I take them to church, Cass?"

"Whatever." He could take the girls. Just so he didn't pester her to go.

CHAPTER THIRTY-SIX

Cassie breathed a sigh of relief when Jon and the girls left the house the next Sunday morning for church. There had been lots of grumbling and complaining but Jon had remained firm. She could tell from the look in his eyes he wanted her to come. There was no way she was going to start that. She didn't need a crutch.

She needed to stay busy so she didn't think about gambling. She decided she'd clean the house from top to bottom and then put a roast in the oven for when the trio got home. She picked up the miscellaneous objects her family had left lying around and put them back where they belonged. She scrubbed sinks and toilets, made beds and dusted. She vacuumed the carpet. She mopped the floors and took out the garbage.

Energized, she went into the kitchen and cleaned out the refrigerator, making faces at the wilted celery, tired lettuce, and mushy cucumbers. She cleaned off counter tops and emptied the dishwasher. After wiping down the stove and oven, she sat down for a cup of tea, just as her cell phone rang.

Who would be calling me on a Sunday morning?
"Hello."
"Hello, Cassie, it's Lorna. I just called to see how you're doing."

Sweat formed on Cassie's hands and her heart thrummed. She hadn't spoken to Lorna since she'd been terminated from Bigelows. No way did she want Lorna nosing around in her life.

"I'm good. How 'bout you?" Cassie did her best to sound upbeat.

"The kids are growing like weeds. and Stan's busier than ever, but we're good."

"How are things at Bigelows?"

"Over the last year, sales have increased. And we're opening two new stores out west."

"You must be pleased."

"I am."

Seconds passed, and neither Cassie nor Lorna spoke. "I miss you, Cassie. I miss seeing your face at work every day." Lorna cleared her throat. "And I miss our friendship."

Anger and sadness churned around in Cassie's stomach at the same time. "Yeah, well ..."

"I'd love to go out to lunch with you sometime."

"You know how it is. My schedule's pretty busy with Jon, the girls, and work."

"Oh? Where are you working?"

Cassie thought quickly. "I work at Deva's Staging. We stage homes." *The lies come so easily.*

"Sounds interesting."

"Yeah. Well, I gotta go, Lorna. I want to get a roast in the oven. Thanks for calling."

"Nice talking to you, Cassie. If you're ever available for lunch, I'd like that."

"We'll see. Bye for now."

Cassie disconnected the call quickly, her finger touching the phone's screen as if it was a hot potato. Why was Lorna calling now? She scrunched her eyes together. When she opened them, a tear trickled down her cheek. Hearing

HOPE DOESN'T DISAPPOINT

Lorna's voice had brought up so many things she didn't want to think about. Now her good day had been ruined. She picked up her cold tea, tossed it down the sink, and looked at the kitchen clock. She needed to get that roast ready.

In a small bowl, she combined olive oil with herbs, salt, and pepper, then rubbed it over the roast. She cut up potatoes and carrots, placed them around the roast, and put everything into the oven. Hopefully it would be ready by the time her family arrived home.

At 12:30 p.m., she heard the garage door rise. The door opened and she heard some rustling in the hallway.

"Hey, something smells good. What are we having?" Anne-Marie bounced into the kitchen, followed by Jesse.

"Roast beef, potatoes, and carrots."

Jon came in and sniffed the air. "Did you say roast beef?"

Cassie nodded.

"When will it be ready?"

"Half an hour or so."

"Great. I'm famished."

The girls got drinks out of the refrigerator and headed to the family room. No one said anything about church. Curiosity got the better of Cassie. "So how was church?"

"Not as bad as we thought it would be," Anne-Marie said over her shoulder before leaving the room.

She hadn't expected that answer.

Later that night, after the girls were in bed, Cassie sat at her computer, catching up on emails. Jon came in and sat in the chair beside her.

"Lorna Nelson called me today," Cassie said.

Keep it offhand. Casual.

Jon blinked in surprise. "Really? She called?"

Cassie shrugged. "I kept it short."

"Why do you think she called?"

"She said she wanted to see how I was doing." Cassie crossed her arms over her chest. "She makes out to be my friend. Some friend. What kind of a friend fires you?"

Jon didn't say anything. Cassie wondered what he was thinking.

He turned sideways and shifted her chair so they faced each other. "Let's not talk about Lorna." He reached out and took her hands in his. Cassie eyed him quizzically.

"You know I love you, right?"

"I do."

Jon reached into his pocket, pulled out a black box, and opened it. Inside, an emerald cut diamond ring sparkled, shooting prisms of light in all directions. Cassie's jaw dropped.

"You thought I didn't notice, didn't you?"

Cassie nodded, her eyes on her husband.

"I'm guessing, but I think you pawned the first one I gave you."

Cassie hung her head as she felt shame wash over her. "I did."

He slipped the ring on Cassie's finger. It fit perfectly. Seconds passed as she stared at the glittering diamond, moving it back and forth on her finger.

"You're quiet. How come?"

"I certainly don't deserve this. I'm wondering why you got it for me."

"What do you mean?"

"Well, I know appearances are important to you. It must bother you for people to see your wife doesn't have an engagement ring on her finger."

Jon backed his chair away from her. "How could you say something like that? I just told you I love you."

"Love has strings attached sometimes."

"Why do you always look for an ulterior motive in everything I do?"

Cassie stared. "Because there usually is one."

Jon stood up so fast the chair almost tipped backward. Anger and hurt flashed in his eyes.

"You're something else, Cass. Sometimes I don't get you. I'm trying, but I'm not having much success. There are days I wonder if I really know you at all." He shoved the chair and it thumped against the desk as it rolled underneath.

Without another word he stormed from the room, banging the door behind him.

CHAPTER THIRTY-SEVEN

Cassie had just settled in the chair by the family room window with a book when Jon pulled a piece of paper out of his back pocket and laid it on the couch where he'd been watching TV.

"What's this, Cassie?"

"What's what?" She got up and looked at the piece of paper. "It's a receipt from the casino." She picked it up and waved it in the air. "Have you been snooping in my coat pockets again?"

Jon didn't answer.

"You're paranoid." She peered at the receipt more closely. "Did you look at the date on it, Sherlock? It's from two months ago."

Jon grabbed the paper from her and scrutinised it. "You're right."

Cassie threw her hands in the air and paced back and forth like an angry cat.

"I'm so tired of you checking up on me. You stopped for a while after you talked to Dan, but now you're right back at it. What are you afraid of? That I'm going to gamble away more money and hock that fancy engagement ring you gave me? We said in our therapy sessions we'd work on trusting each other. You're not keeping your end of the bargain."

Jon stared at his wife.

"I've had it," she said. "I can't take you inspecting everything I do. You're making me a nervous wreck. I'm not sleeping, and I've lost my appetite."

She left the room and made a beeline up the stairs to the bedroom. When she reached it, she rushed in, slammed the door, and fell face down on the bed as hot, angry tears began to fall. Now that she was back home, would things always be tense between her and Jon? Would gambling always dog her steps whether she was in the casino or not?

When her tears finally subsided, Cassie sat up. She noticed Jon's Bible on his night table, picked it up, and returned to the bed with half a mind to start tearing out the pages. She opened the Bible to find a good chapter to start ripping out, and encountered the book of John. Instead of beginning her destruction immediately, she began to read. At the fourth chapter, she saw the title "A Samaritan Woman Meets Her Messiah."

She read the chapter through once, then read it again.

On the third time through, Cassie stopped, lost in thought. The nameless Samaritan woman hadn't led a stellar life. Perhaps she'd had so many husbands because she was promiscuous. Perhaps she'd never found someone to truly love her. Obviously she was scorned by the city folk, since she went alone at the hottest time of the day to draw water. But Jesus took the opportunity to talk to her, to reveal to her that he was the Messiah.

One of the verses wedged itself in her mind, the verse about it being necessary for Jesus to go through Samaria. Jesus went out of his way to meet with this one errant woman, and not just any woman, but an outcast Samaritan woman.

It was socially unfit for Jesus to talk to such a woman, but he did it anyway. He loved her, accepted her, and set her free. And through her testimony, many others came to believe in him.

Cassie bowed her head and thought about the Samaritan woman, then about herself. The two of them had done bad things, and yet the Samaritan woman was forgiven.

If Jesus loved her with all her sins, could he love me? Would he forgive me?

She'd had enough of struggling on her own. Deva was right. The more she strained, the worse things got. It was worth a try, anyway.

"Dear Jesus," she prayed, "I really don't know why I've resisted you this long. I guess I have a rebellious, stubborn spirit. The fact you spent time with this Samaritan woman—not with a rich person, not a priest, but a wayward woman—this speaks to my heart. I've done so many wrong things. I ask you to forgive me. Jon and Deva have told me that through your death and resurrection, I can have forgiveness and eternal life."

She stopped and took a deep breath. She hoped she was being heard. "Jon told me you love me more than I can comprehend. All my life I've been looking for someone who loves me just for who I am." Sudden tears filled her eyes, and she gulped back a sob. "Please fill this emptiness in my heart with your love and understanding. And thank you for removing the burden of gambling from me and freeing my soul." After a moment of silence, not knowing what else to say, she murmured an awkward "Amen."

When she lifted her head, she felt strange inside, until she recognized what she was feeling was pure, true joy. She'd known happiness off and on in the past, based on her life's circumstances, but not this. This joy felt like water bubbling up inside her, like the gushing well of fresh water Jesus had described to the Samaritan woman. She wondered if that woman so long ago had experienced the same joy she sensed now. Nothing she'd ever known before could match it.

When Jon finally came up to bed, Cassie got up and grabbed him.

"I've got something to tell you."

She sat on the bed and motioned for him to sit beside her. After their previous exchange, he seemed reluctant.

"Sit, Jon, please? It's important."

He plunked down on the bed, making sure to keep a few inches between them. "What?" he said, his tone dull.

She took his hand. "I prayed. I talked to Jesus and asked him to fill up my empty spots and live in my heart. I asked him, and he came."

Slowly he turned to look at her. "You wouldn't joke about this, would you?"

She shook her head and held up the Bible. "The story of the Samaritan woman?"

"I know the one. It's in the chapter after Jesus talks to Nicodemus."

"Well, I read it, and it really spoke to me. Jesus went out of his way for a wayward Samaritan woman who apparently botched things up in her life. Sorta like me." Her feet swung back and forth over the edge of the bed, like a child's. "Even though Jesus knew all about her past, he still loved her and even told her he was the Messiah. She quibbled with him at first, but then she believed him and accepted his love, and she went and told the whole city to come and meet him."

Jon moved a little closer.

"If Jesus cared that much about a shady lady and forgave her, then I knew he cared about me and would forgive me. I prayed, and told him I was sorry for what I'd done, and asked him to forgive me, and then I asked him into my heart." Her words tumbled out in a rush of excitement. Her eyes shone. "I could almost hear him unlock the chains around me. I heard them snap open. I stepped out of them, and now I'm free."

She raised her arms in the air, reaching toward heaven. Jon couldn't help himself, raising his own arms in the air beside her.

"Praise the Lord," he said fervently. "He answered your prayer. He answered our prayer."

They climbed into bed, cuddled together like spoons, and slept the sleep of the blessed.

CHAPTER THIRTY-EIGHT

Jon and Cassie sat beside each other at their kitchen table, glasses of iced tea in front of them. Anne-Marie and Jesse were already in bed. The overhead lighting cast a soft glow on the center of the table. Outside, a stiff breeze made the open window rattle, and Cassie wondered if they were in for a torrential summer downpour. Humid air circulated in the room. She noticed Jesse's last report card lying on the counter and picked it up.

"I was happy to see Jesse's motivation improved near the end of school," she said. "She pulled a few of those C's up to B's."

Jon took the card and glanced over it. "I told you she didn't need a private school. Your hard work with her paid off."

The edges of Cassie's mouth curved upward. "And yours. Using games helped her with her spelling."

"Jesse love games. She takes after me on that." He took a sip of his drink. "We're getting closer to having enough money for a down payment on a house."

Cassie gave him a surprised look. "Really?"

"Yes, ma'am."

"How long do you think it will be before we have enough?"

"I'd say six to eight months."

"That's exciting. It gives us something to look forward to."

Jon nodded. "Speaking of time passing, how long has it been since you last gambled?"

"Four months."

"You must be tempted sometimes." He put an elbow on the table and rested his chin in his hand. Cassie took a swallow of tea and set her glass down.

"I am. The statistics say eighty to ninety percent of individuals entering recovery from addiction will relapse during the first year. Not great news."

He shook his head. "It isn't." Getting up, he went to the fridge and took out a pitcher of water. "My tea's a little too sweet. I'm going to add some water. Would you like some for yours?

Cassie shook her head.

When he sat down, she traced her finger around the rim of her glass for several seconds before speaking. Through the window, she saw a bolt of lightning pierce the sky, followed by a crack of thunder. The storm was getting closer.

"Certain things trigger me. If I'm feeling bored, I crave the thrill of winning a jackpot. When I see gambling sites advertised on television or elsewhere, adrenalin starts pulsing through my veins. And if I'm lonely or sad, I want to head to the casino or my computer."

"What do you do?"

She sighed. "I try to think about you and the girls and how much you mean to me. If I'm feeling lonely, I call Deva when I'm not at work. I also try to do something physical, like cleaning or going for a walk."

"That explains why the house is so clean." Jon winked.

She poked him in the ribs. "I'd say the most important thing I'm learning to do is to read God's Word."

HOPE DOESN'T DISAPPOINT

"What sections do you like to read?"

"I'm so new to this Bible reading thing, but the other day, in one of the books of Peter, it says Satan is poised to pounce and likes to catch us napping. Because of that, I need to keep a cool head, stay alert, and keep my guard up. And I have to remember God gets the last word."

"I like the part about God getting the last word."

"Me too. The world we live in has such warped philosophies." Cassie banged her fist on the table. "In a sense, you could say gambling is a warped philosophy. The philosophy of gambling says I'll have fun, win money, and meet the deepest emotional needs of my heart. But I'm learning only Jesus can meet those needs."

"So true."

Outside, rain poured from the sky onto the roof, the gutters, and into the open kitchen window.

Jon closed the window and returned to his seat.

"The storm's finally here. It's been so dry the past few weeks. We need the rain."

Cassie nodded and swirled the remains of her tea around the bottom of the glass.

"Is it easy to resist the temptation to gamble?" she mused aloud. "Definitely not. Some days the struggle is harder than others. But when I keep my eyes focused on Jesus, he doesn't disappoint me."

Jon put his arm around Cassie and pulled her closer. "You're a smart lady."

"I married you, right?" She laughed and kissed his cheek. "And sometimes I come to you so we can pray together."

"True." He looked at her tenderly. "Whenever you feel the urge to gamble and want prayer, come to me. Early in the morning or the middle of the night, I don't care. Come and get me."

"I appreciate that."

In the stillness, with only the kitchen clock's beat keeping time with her heart, she found it easier to be honest with Jon. The more he knew, the more supportive he could be. If she kept everything to herself, he had no way to know what she was dealing with.

He sipped from his glass. "Penny for your thoughts."

"I'm just thankful to have you."

He squeezed her hand. "And I'm grateful you're making progress. I can see it."

"Thanks. Some days when the temptation is strong, it's hard for me to tell if I'm making headway."

Jon glanced down at their hands and entwined his fingers with hers. "You are."

They sat in silence, holding hands. After several minutes, Jon stood up.

"It's getting late. Let's go up to bed."

CHAPTER THIRTY-NINE

"What time does it start?" Jesse ran into her parents' bedroom, tucking her tee shirt into her pants.

August had arrived, and the girls would be back at school soon. Cassie stood at the bedroom window. Where had the summer gone? Somehow she needed to catch the days and hold onto them longer. If time continued to fly by, before she knew it, the girls would be attending high school. The thought made her sad and happy at the same time.

In the west, the sun cast a golden glow. It shone through the glass, making a path of light across the floor. For a second, she stared at the thousands of dust particles floating in the air before she turned and looked at Jesse.

"Six-thirty. We have to leave in fifteen minutes." Walking closer to her daughter, she peered more closely and frowned. "I bought you a new blouse, Jess. It's hanging in your closet. Did you see it?"

"I like what I've got on."

"It would mean a lot to me if you wore the new blouse." Jesse scowled.

"Never mind. If you want to wear what you've got on, that's okay." Cassie knew it was important to choose her battles. She didn't want to make this one of them.

"Thanks, Mom. What's it called we're going to?"

"It's a baptism service. Your dad and I will be baptized this evening."

"Is it like when we went to the christening of our neighbor's baby, Lisa, and a priest put water on her head? Is a priest or minister gonna sprinkle water on you?"

Cassie shook her head. "Underneath the floor at the front of the church, there's a tank that will be full of water. There are stairs leading down into the tank. The person being baptized goes into the tank of water."

Jesse's eyebrows shot up. "Do you wear your clothes into the tank?"

"Dad and I will wear our swimsuits under cotton gowns."

"What happens after the person is in the tank of water?"

"Well, Pastor Toussant told us we'll have an opportunity to tell the audience how we came to invite Jesus into our life. He called it giving our testimony. Then he'll ask us if we believe Jesus is the Son of God, that he rose from the dead on the third day, and if we have accepted him as our Savior and Lord. When we answer yes, he dunks us under the water and says he baptizes us in the name of the Father, the Son, and the Holy Ghost. Then he lifts us out of the water."

"How will he manage a big guy like Dad?"

Cassie smiled. "Sometimes two people go into the tank to help each other or because the person being baptized is a special friend."

"Is Dad gonna have two people?"

"Yes. The pastor and Dad's friend from work, Dan Marano, will be in the tank. "A tiny smile formed at the corners of her mouth. "Hopefully they won't drop him in the water."

"What about you?"

Cassie looked down at her clasped fingers. "My boss Deva is going to be with the minister and me."

HOPE DOESN'T DISAPPOINT

Jesse looked thoughtful. "Why are you and Dad doing this?"

"We want to tell everyone we've accepted Jesus as our Savior. It's a symbol. When I go down into the water, it's like me dying to living my life without Jesus. When I'm lifted out of the water, it shows I'm reborn. I'm a new person in him."

"Cool."

※ ※ ※ ※ ※ ※

When they arrived at the church, people were already heading into the auditorium. Cassie could see a metal cover over the baptismal tank and hoped it was not only to keep people from falling in, but to ensure the water stayed warm. She shivered.

A few choir members filed into their seats behind the pulpit. Cassie stared in surprise when she saw her father walking uncertainly into the sanctuary. She had invited him days before, thinking there was only a remote possibility he would attend.

He spotted her and came over.

"I'm not sure what this is all about, Cass," he muttered, "but I'm proud of you."

Cassie whispered back, "I'm really glad you came, Dad. I'm sorry for the way I've treated you, and I want you to know I love you. I've been angry at you for not being there for me, but I haven't been there for you either." Taking a deep breath, she continued. "But that's going to change. We love you, and Jesus loves you, and my prayer is you'll come to know that." She smiled at him. "Jon and I want you to come over for dinner this Friday. Will you?"

Cassie wasn't sure, but she thought she saw tears in her father's eyes. "I'd like that."

"Anne-Marie and Jesse and my boss, Deva, are sitting over there." Cassie pointed. "Why don't you join them?"

He looked hesitant. Cassie waited and breathed a sigh of relief when he walked away from her and joined the trio, pointing back at her as if to say, "She told me to come sit with you." The girls gave him big smiles.

Jon was baptized first. After he shared his testimony, Dan spoke to Jon as they stood in the baptismal tank with the pastor. He encouraged Jon to be all that God created him to be, and reminded him that God's plans were to prosper, not to harm, and to give hope and a future. When Jon came up out of the water, his face glowed.

When it was Cassie's turn, she lifted her eyes and looked out at the congregation.

"My life was a mess," she began. "Satan is a deceiver and a liar. When I started gambling, it seemed like just a fun pastime, but it caught me in a stranglehold." She took a deep breath. "Because of gambling, I nearly lost my husband and children. I did lose my job, and we lost our house. And I very nearly lost my life."

Cassie stopped and lowered her head. Vague memories flooded her mind, memories of ingesting the acetaminophen pills as she sat in her car, hopeless. Then memories of other events intruded, flickering through in kaleidoscopic images—the humiliation of being pushed into a police cruiser as a common criminal, and the terror during her brief time in jail. Bridges burned with family and friends. The fear and despair she found in shelters.

She shook her head to remove the scenes passing behind her eyelids like a silent movie. Then she scanned the audience. "But God …"

A tear trickled down her cheek, and she swiped it away with the back of her hand. "I love those words—but God. Through events and people, God led me to Jesus. Now, each day as I trust in him, he delivers me from the bondage of gambling."

The congregation applauded, and she smiled. "All the praise, all the applause goes to God."

Deva stood from her pew in the auditorium, her Bible in her hand.

"Cassie." She paused for a moment. "The book of Isaiah says even though the mountains and hills crumble, God's love for you will never end, and he will keep forever his promise of peace, because he loves you.

"A little lesson about the word 'peace.' It comes from the Hebrew word shalom, and signifies completeness, wholeness, health, restoration. So, Cassie, God's will for you and your family is to know his peace and everything it entails, no matter what your circumstances. And the twenty-third Psalm says because the Lord is your shepherd, you lack nothing. In Jesus, you and Jon have everything you need. Never forget that."

"Thank you, Deva."

As Cassie gazed into the audience, she thought she saw a tear glistening on Anne-Marie's cheek. She prayed inwardly her girls would consider and remember what they heard on this night.

Deva set her Bible down on the pew, walked to the front of the auditorium, and slowly climbed the stairs to the platform. She wore a long multi-colored skirt and a crisp white blouse, her hair bunched in a messy bun on the top of her head. Without hesitating, she descended into the water and waded to Cassie's side.

"I know I've already spoken," she said, "but I got more to say."

The audience twittered, and Cassie smiled.

"Because of what Jesus has done for us, we can go right into his throne room and ask him for help when we need it. That's like being able to go to the Queen of England and asking her for what we need. Only it's a lot better, because she's only human, and God is God." Deva reached out and took Cassie's hand. "It's amazing. The God who runs the universe said we can come to him for help.

"Before I end—and I will end—" Deva paused and winked at Cassie, "I wanna bless you and Jon with the blessing in the book of Numbers, the one God told Aaron to use when he blessed the children of Israel. It goes like this."

Deva lifted her chin. "May the Lord bless you and protect you. May the Lord smile on you and be gracious to you. May the Lord show you his favor and give you his peace." She stopped and looked out at the audience. "I like the paraphrase that says, '… May the Lord's face radiate with joy because of you.'"

She turned back to Cassie. "Jesus is happy and radiating with joy because of you." In their soggy clothing, Deva and Cassie hugged each other tightly.

Pastor Toussant stepped forward and smiled. "Thank you for encouraging all of us, Deva. Now let's baptize Cassie together."

The pastor stood on one side of Cassie and Deva on the other.

"Cassie, based on the confession of your faith in the Lord Jesus and your desire to follow him into the waters of baptism, I baptize you in the name of the Father, the Son, and the Holy Spirit."

Together, the pastor and her friend lowered her into the water and lifted her up again. Cassie, water streaming from her face and hair, looked up, and flung both arms heavenward.

"In Jesus, I am free!"

The audience erupted into applause. They stood, clapping their hands and praising God. The choir launched into the first verse of "Amazing Grace" as she exited the tank.

Later, after the baptized ones had changed into dry clothes and everyone had come into the large fellowship hall for refreshments, Anne-Marie approached her mom.

"I don't know what it was, Mom," she said, her earnest eyes peering into Cassie's, "but I was happy tonight when you said you were free, and I heard the singing and clapping during the service."

Jesse came bounding over with a large piece of cake, icing on the corners of her mouth. "I felt good tonight, Mom. Happy and not all jumbled up inside like I do sometimes."

Joyful and elated, Cassie gave them each a tight hug.

Then Jon's parents approached her. "Even though we didn't understand everything, we enjoyed the service. Maybe we'll come back."

On a wave of gratitude, Cassie embraced them. "You've both been so good to us, and you stuck with us, even during the rough times. We love you very much. We'd like nothing better than for you to come to church with us."

The next day, as sunlight shone through the kitchen window and made shadows across the table where Cassie sat, praise overflowed in her heart. She took another sip of her tea and glanced at the clock on the wall. The girls would be home from school soon.

"I'd better start preparing dinner," she muttered, reluctant to get up from the table.

As she assembled her ingredients for homemade lasagna, she remembered a verse in Isaiah about children being taught by the Lord and having great peace. She knew that someday, even though they weren't receptive now, her daughters would experience God's peace. Joy filled Cassie's heart, and then overflowed into song.

A few minutes later Cassie heard backpacks and jackets clatter onto the bench in the entryway. Giggles added to the clamor. She met them in the front hall.

"Were you two laughing at my rendition of 'Amazing Grace'?" She did her best to look and sound offended.

"No, Mom. We wouldn't laugh at you."

"Then what?"

"We think the mom who sings out of tune is a whole lot better than the one who gambled."

The girls raced into the kitchen, looking for snacks. A tide of hope washed through Cassie as she followed them. She'd come so close to losing everything, so close to drowning in that dark place. Jesus had offered her his love and his lifeline, and she'd grabbed onto them both. Now her trust was in Christ. She knew her hope in him was eternal. Her hope in him would never disappoint her.

ABOUT THE AUTHOR

DORALYN MOORE has a Master of Education degree from the University of Toronto and over thirty years experience in social services, working with diverse populations. For many years, she has been involved in Christian ministry, both as a home group leader and as a lay pastor. Moore lives with her husband in a small community east of Toronto, Canada. Their two boys are now married with their own families. Moore and her husband have five beautiful grandchildren.

Manufactured by Amazon.ca
Bolton, ON